THE LOSS OF THE
BURYING GROUND

THE LOSS OF THE BURYING GROUND

J. ANDERSON COATS

CANDLEWICK PRESS

Copyright © 2024 by J. Anderson Coats
Frontispiece illustration copyright © 2024 by Jeff Langevin
Illustration of chess piece on pp. 23, 46, 107,
and 217 copyright © 2024 by ValterDesign/Shutterstock.com
Illustration of cage on p. 277 copyright © 2024 by rangsan paidaen/Shutterstock.com

First edition 2024

Library of Congress Catalog Card Number pending
ISBN 978-1-5362-3238-7

24 25 26 27 28 29 APS 10 9 8 7 6 5 4 3 2 1

Printed in Humen, Dongguan, China

This book was typeset in Chaparral, Bembo, and Futura.

Candlewick Press
99 Dover Street
Somerville, Massachusetts 02144

www.candlewick.com

To Iris,
who is becoming

THE ISLAND

CORA

THE FIRST THREE things I realize:

My head is killing me.

I have never been this sore.

I am soaking wet.

But when I peel my eyes open and take in an expanse of golden sand that ends in a thick line of tangly trees, it's a long, waterlogged moment before I realize a fourth thing. A thing I was hoping was all a really, *really* bad dream.

I'm not on the deck of the *Burying Ground*. There's nothing left of either peace delegation. No sign of the treaty that was finally going to end the War of Ariminthian Aggression. A massive storm really did turn a forty-gun warship to sawdust and toothpicks beneath our feet.

Then it capsized what was left like a paper boat in a bathtub.

Then it flung those pieces into one another and into us while we fought the surf and lost.

I push myself up. Onto my backside. My muscles scream and my sunburned skin crunches and I suck a breath through my teeth.

The ocean stretches without measure in front of me. Calm now. Cheerful and rolling, swishing toward me up the sand in a gentle sheet. Empty of anything and so blue it hurts my head. The sort of thing a little kid would draw.

I squinch my eyes shut. When I open them again, I'll be in my room. Lying on my bed. All my stuff nearby. My books. My sewing basket. My precious packet from the war work placement center containing everything I'd need to convince my parents that working at a fish hatchery would be *very* patriotic, and it was merely a coincidence that it happened to have coed dorms and require two hours' travel to get there.

Merely a coincidence that it happened to be somewhere adults had better things to do than hover like mosquitoes looking for a patch of bare skin to stab and stab again. *How late will you be? Will their parents be home? That skirt is awfully short.*

It doesn't work. My shoulder is still pressing into sand, not the soft faded quilt I've had forever. The sun is baking down, and there's nothing nearby but a scatter of broken shells and a few strings of seaweed in an uneven, haphazard line.

A slow, cold feeling seeps through me.

I'm on a beach that curls away and out of sight in both directions, empty of people and animals. There's chirring and cheeping from the trees behind me, and all at once the *shush-shush* of the water is unnerving.

"Hello?" I croak, and gah, it even hurts to *talk*.

—screaming my throat raw grappling for a plank but none of them hold me up a wave shoves me under mouth full of—

Slowly, gritting my teeth, I climb to my feet. My bare feet. My bare—oh crackers—my bare *everything*. The only clothing the storm left me is the cute lacy camisole and underwear that Kess dared me to buy at the dress shop a week before she moved away, that my mother found while cleaning and confiscated and gave me an earful about.

I sneaked those skivvies back out of her closet, and I wear them whenever I need to be more like Kess. Even though it's been a few years and they don't fit so well anymore. Maybe no one else can see them, but I know they're there.

Right now my underwear is all anyone can see, and there's nothing nearby to cover up with. No scrap of sailcloth or even a piece of wood, and I don't think my father will have seen this much of me since I was in diapers. That's bad enough, but then there are the Duran cabinet secretaries, their assistants—

And oh. It's possible that Ariminthians will be here, too. The royal family or their servants, or perhaps sailors from the *Burying Ground*.

If it wasn't for them—*all of them*—there would be no war and therefore no need for a peace treaty and definitely no need to hold the signing on a ship in neutral waters.

I'd better find the Duran delegation. Right now.

"Hello?" This time I get some volume. Not quite a shout, but the best I'm going to do till I wash the sand out of my throat. "Anyone? Dad? Mom?"

The ocean goes *shush-shush*. The trees go *chirrrrrrr-cheecheechee*.

I move slowly toward the tree line. Toward the shade. I move slow because my head is swimming and pounding and swim-pounding, and I am not thinking about what I'll do if there's no sign of my parents. Or any of the Duran diplomats.

Or anyone.

There's a big smooth rock where the sand changes color, and I sink onto it. It's blissfully cool against my bare legs, and the relief it brings helps me push aside—for just a little longer—some very basic things that I will soon have to reckon with.

Like that I've been shipwrecked on an island in barely charted waters where pirates are known to prowl. I have no food, no water, no clothing, no shelter, and no idea when someone will come get me.

The *Burying Ground* is currently at the bottom of the ocean, and there's no way to know who survived its sinking besides me.

If anyone.

Which means the entire peace delegation may have drowned. Our cabinet secretaries and the whole Ariminthian royal family.

Which means the war that's been going on my whole life—

—that took both my brothers and too many of my friends, that left my mother bedridden for nearly a year—

—that gives my parents way too many reasons to hover over me—

—that's shaped and governed every choice I've ever made—

—that war just may have gotten a whole lot further from won.

VIVIENNE

I WATCHED HER drown.

Princess Aubrielle Melisande Felicity Tiralie Vivienne of Ariminthia thrashed and struggled in the churning gray-black surf, grabbing at broken spars and lunging for jagged pieces of the foredeck, the rail, the topsail yard. I clung to a crate and shouted to her—

—*my lady, hold on, I'm coming*—

—but the roar of the storm caught my desperate cry and chewed it to bits just as a wave rose behind her, its rush lost in the gale, and pushed her down, down and down, not giving her time to scream, to pray, to beg.

The sea does not give back what it takes.

So I let go of the crate. I would go down, too. Wherever she was, I would be. Whatever became of her, I would join her there.

But the sea is strange. It has a plan for each of us, and its ways are not for us to know. Not kings, not princesses, and definitely not the likes of me.

I remind myself of this again and again while I lie crumpled on this stretch of golden sand, while one day becomes the next. The sea has put me here. There's something that it wants. Something I'm meant to do.

So I build her a shrine.

I walk this stretch of sand till I have sixteen smooth stones. One for each year of her age. Each is the size of my palm and pure white.

Then I move through the jungle till I have five flowers. One for each year I've been her lady's maid. Each is weighed down with dew like it weeps for her already.

I carefully place them—first the stones, then the flowers—on the mound I created from handful on handful of sand. One grain for every time I'd willingly die if it meant she could be alive here, on this beach, scanning the treacherously calm water for the ship that even now must be on its way to rescue her.

The sea is strange. There are few things that are not within its power, but not even the sea can make a ship fall to pieces like what befell the *Burying Ground*, like the very nails and joints turned to mist.

That takes an act of sabotage.

We were all searched before we embarked. Right there on the wharf of the neutral port. Pockets emptied and trunks

unpacked. Even the king and his consort submitted to such base treatment for the sake of peace. Representatives from our side searched the Durans' belongings, and the Durans searched ours, in full view of one another.

The terms were clear: No weapons. No wires. No jewelry, even. Nothing that might be harmful, or could be made harmful through craft.

The Durans never wanted peace, though. That is plain enough now. War is deeply profitable for that sordid lot, with their workshops and their machines and their constant stream of fleeting, malleable printed words.

I sit beside the shrine as the shadows from the trees shift and lengthen. As my belly grows growly and my skin itchy from the salt.

Without her to do for, I don't know what to do. Since I was eleven years old, I have awakened on a little pallet at the foot of her bed and made myself useful. I draw her baths and mend her dresses and polish her bracelets and fetch her tea.

I keep her secrets.

The sun inches deep into the sea and streaks the sky with bands of glorious color. I shiver in the growing twilight.

I *drew* her baths. I *mended* her dresses. My mistress is dead. The Durans have killed her, and someday, somehow, they will pay.

CORA

I CAN'T SIT here all day. Sitting won't get me rescued.

More importantly, it won't get me water.

I walk up the beach, swaying a little, picking up useful things as I go. Then I follow my footprints back to where I woke up. For some silly reason, I don't want to lose track of this place.

Now I perch on my rock and look over my findings. A salt-stiffened length of rope that's fraying at one end, a canvas sea bag with *Alivarda* stenciled on the side, a black leather valise that's locked up tight, and a tattery piece of what might be sailcloth.

Things that have to be from the *Burying Ground*.

What I didn't find was any sign at all of another person. No footprints. No fire-blackened rocks. No recent signs. No old ones.

At least that means there are no pirates.

It was not smart to do all that walking. My tongue feels like sawdust, and my headache is filling my skull with the kind of pounding that's hard to think through.

"I only went up and down the beach," I say aloud, to myself and my findings. "I hardly went into the trees at all. That's probably where everyone is. That's probably where water is."

But the jungle is thick and dense, and there are all sorts of strange chirring and whooing sounds that are most likely birds, but not birds I recognize. There's also a constant low hum of insects that could bite and sting and give me diseases I can't imagine.

Out on the beach I feel tiny, like a single pea left on a plate. So much water stretching everywhere and the sky above that same blue, curving down into a dome to hold me in.

Back there, though. I could walk ten steps and be lost.

"Hello?" I shout. "Somebody? *Anybody?*"

Please. Just answer. Please, someone just be here.

Tears wick down my sunburned cheeks, and I swipe at them and crackers but I don't even care about the hatchery right now. I wish I was home. I wish I'd never agreed to come at all.

I wish Dura had just won the war with one big battle that had made Ariminthia surrender. Something decisive and crushing, none of this negotiation business. So everyone knew what was what, who won and who lost.

Who was right and who was wrong.

"I'll keep talking," I say. "Someone will hear me. They'll come find me. Then we can figure out how to get rescued. But for now, I need food and water."

I don't move, though. Instead, I squint at my findings. I already tried the lock on the valise with no luck, but the sea bag is only held closed by a drawstring.

Alivarda is an Ariminthian name.

There's a bit of good in today, then. I never thought I'd get a chance to plunder something of the enemy's.

The knot in the drawstring is caked with salt, but I pick at it with my fingernails and a pointy piece of wood I find near the rock. "I'm going to say you drowned, Alivarda. I'm not sorry, either. This whole war is your fault. Every last Ariminthian's fault. It's your fault that my brothers are dead. Your fault that kids have to leave school to do war work. Your fault there's rationing and shortages."

It's nice, having the knot to pick open. If I'm forcing this knot, I'm not thinking about food and water. I'm not thinking about how in order to get those things, I'm going to have to walk into those trees. I'll have to leave this rock. This beach.

I'm not thinking how there's a very good chance I'm alone here.

I'm almost disappointed when the drawstring finally loosens and I can open the sea bag. On top there's some wadded-up salt-stiff linen that cricks and cracks apart and turns into a tunic and trousers. I hold the trousers against my lower half and oh.

They look like they'd fit me.

Alivarda wasn't a sailor or a marine. He was a cabin boy. A kid my age.

"I'm going to wear your kit, Alivarda," I say as I pull on the trousers and cinch the drawstring belt around my waist. "Somehow I don't think you're going to need it anymore. And if you do, if you walk up that beach or out of those trees and want it back, I will fight you for it. You will not enjoy the experience, and you will lose."

It's pure trash talk—there's no way I could beat up someone whose job is to climb ropes and haul heavy cloth—but it feels right to say. It feels right to take something from the enemy when they've taken so much from me.

There's a leather waterskin that takes up most of the sea bag. It's full and sloshy, and I pry out the stopper and guzzle mouthfuls of warm, stale water so fast, I almost choke.

The waterskin is half-empty when I remember from invasion readiness training that you can live only a few days without fresh water. When Sergeant Bale's calm, evenhanded voice in my head starts describing exactly what happens to your body as you're dying of dehydration.

I stuff the stopper back into the bung and put the waterskin down gently, then I turn my back because that makes it easier to keep from drinking it dry.

At the bottom of the bag is a jackknife. The blade folds out with the smallest *scriff* of salt. It's short, the length of my finger, but razor-sharp. There are faint strands of rope caught between the blade and the handle, and I pluck them out one by one.

No one on the *Burying Ground* was supposed to have any weapons, but it's just like an Ariminthian to ignore rules they don't like.

Anyway, the knife is mine now, same as the clothes. The linen is stiff, damp, and smells like old closets. It's like wearing sandpaper, which lights up my sunburned skin in a sheet of raw agony, but sitting here in Alivarda's tunic and trousers after a few drinks of his water suddenly makes more things seem possible.

Like walking into the jungle.

Alivarda's water won't last forever. Exploring is the only way to find more. Food, too. Maybe the rest of the Duran delegation.

So I tie one end of the rope I found to a little palm sapling near my rock, hoist the coils over my shoulder, and start walking.

Ten steps in and already it's much cooler. Pleasantly so. The chirring and whooing echo, and I'm glad for the rope as I spool it out. It would be so easy to get lost here when all these trees look alike.

I think I hear a trickle of water, so I edge my way through dense jungle brush, watching where I step. Soon I come upon a bank of bushes with round dark berries dangling in clumps. My mouth waters, but I remember from invasion readiness training that it's worse to eat something bad than it is to go hungry.

I should keep walking.

The berries are a deep purple, almost black, about the size of my thumb. They remind me of daleberries, but islands on the high seas might as well be the moon. I'd never even seen the ocean before the *Burying Ground*.

Daleberries sure are good. Juicy, too. Juicy like the water I can't stop thinking about.

I should *keep walking*.

But I also remember from training that blue and purple fruits are the least likely to be poisonous. *Break it open and touch your tongue to it*, Sergeant Bale told us. *Wait ten minutes. If there's no burning or stinging, take a small bite. In half an hour, if there's no vomiting, no diarrhea, no off feelings, it's probably safe to eat.*

I pick a berry and split it with my thumbnail. The inside is a familiar pale purple. I touch my tongue to it and it's pleasantly sweet, and all I can think is *grab them, eat them, cram every last one into your mouth now now now.*

I don't, though. I sit calmly, like Sergeant Bale said to.

I have no way to tell the time.

So I start talking. "Well, Dad, I don't know if you and Mom are on this island with me. Maybe you are, but if you're not, you don't have to worry about me. The rescue ships are probably on the way right now. They must be. Everyone will figure something's not right when the *Burying Ground* doesn't turn up at the neutral port when it should."

I prod the berry again and add, "Honestly, Dad, I feel like this is the first time I've managed to get a word in edgewise since, well, ever. Good chat."

I laugh because I mean it to be funny, but my throat still aches, and once I've said it, it doesn't sound as funny as it did in my head.

"Once we're rescued, well . . ." Berry juice is running down my hand. "Hard to know what will happen, right? I mean, you were always saying it would take a miracle to even get the Ariminthians to the bargaining table. You were all, *Their whole country is full of pompous aristocrats who'd rather fight to the last peasant than admit defeat.*"

I wait for him to oh so patiently remind me how editorials work, how the whole point is convincing people to see things your way, or reminding them how smart they are if they already agree with you, and I would do well to pay attention.

He doesn't, though. Because he's not here.

So I say, louder, "If that's true, though, I don't get why we gave them all those concessions. We agreed to sign the treaty on a ship at sea. We agreed to the searches before boarding. Heck, we even let them build that ship special so they'd know there was no funny business!"

Those weren't the only things we agreed to. The Ariminthians insisted that the entire Duran delegation bring their families on board. Anything less would be evidence that the whole thing was a setup and we intended sabotage.

But at least Parliament pushed back on that, and finally it was agreed that all sides would bring their families. The prime minister and four top cabinet secretaries who would sign for us, and the entire Ariminthian royal family—the king, his consort, the crown prince, and the three princesses.

"All you had to do was let me go to the hatchery," I whisper.

"I could be there right now. Helping the war effort. Feeding the fish. Meeting cute biologists."

Learning that both my parents had been lost at sea and there was a nonzero chance I was an orphan.

My heart hurts. It could be the berry. But I know it's not.

"Only I had to go on the *Burying Ground*, didn't I?" I ask my dad quietly. "I had to go or else you couldn't."

Dad never said a word about what that moment would mean. That being the newspaperman chosen by random lottery to witness and report on the signing of the peace treaty so many had bled for would not only make his career and likely put him in the history books, but give him a way to get past my brothers dying so horribly.

"All things considered, it *would* have been better if they'd picked someone else," I tell my dad in a voice I mean to be teasing. "I know, I know. The Ariminthians didn't want any reporters in the first place. Can't challenge their precious chronicle that only records the Crown's version of things, but excluding you personally was an unreasonable request, one they had no right to make. Blah-blah threat assessment. Blah-blah the kind of paranoid rantings we've come to expect from them. If they planned to insist on a reporter who hadn't lost someone in the war, they were going to wait a long freaking time." I laugh grimly. "Maybe that was the point."

Several cabinet secretaries thought my dad should have bowed out when the Ariminthians kicked up a fuss, even though the royal envoys wouldn't give a solid reason. That the Duran delegation digging in its heels on the subject would make the enemy even more suspicious.

But the prime minister had made a big deal about the nation-wide lottery, how it would ensure both fairness and security, and he stood behind the randomizing. Especially when the alternate was single, no family to risk, and that would look even worse.

"If the royal family all drowned, that would make things better for us," I say to my juice-sticky hands. "There wouldn't be a king, so there'd be no one to tell the nobles what to do. We could just walk in and take over."

It feels good to say, but I know it's not going to happen. Back when I went to school, we learned that the king has three brothers of legitimate royal blood, which is an Ariminthian way of saying one of them will get to be the new king, even though he's done nothing to deserve it or earn it other than being born to the right people.

The king's brothers are serving as fleet commanders, and for a while Parliament hoped at least one of them could be promised something that would make him turn on the others, or maybe help our side on the sly, or at least do nothing and not help anyone.

They were wrong.

Those were bad years.

"And Mom, I guess this means there's no way you're signing that permission form for the hatchery now." I laugh halfway. "If you didn't want to let me out of your sight before—crackers, you're probably going to fit me with a leash. It's not that I don't like the nursery. It's just hard to keep friends, you know? When you hang out with a bunch of little kids all day handing out cups of milk and tacking up finger paintings, and everyone else is doing night shifts at the lumberyard or the metal smithy."

And before she can start, I add, "Yes, I *know* it's important work, and people rely on the nurseries to take care of their kids so they can do their part for the war effort. I *get* it. I *know* it's not patriotic to complain, and I am not complaining. I don't *mind* doing my part. *All right?*"

No one tells me to watch my smart mouth. My mom's not here and neither is my dad, and I'm waiting to see whether my guts are going to turn inside out from tasting that berry.

You don't have to worry about me.

No one's hovering now, and if I get rescued—*when* I get rescued—it's going to be because I *stayed calm* and *took my bearings* and everything else Sergeant Bale said to do.

All the newspapers in Dura are going to want to know how I did it, what it was like on the island, how I managed to stay alive. I could give speeches. Maybe there'll be parades. Maybe even a medal from Parliament.

Not just anyone will be able to say they're a survivor of the *Burying Ground*.

I clear my throat. Still sore. Still sandy. "Well, it looks like I haven't died. I'm going to take a bite."

So I do. I pop the probably-a-daleberry into my mouth. It's sweet and pleasant and juicy and delicious.

I don't wait half an hour. Sorry, Sergeant Bale. I pick handfuls and gobble them down. I lose track of how long I stand at that bush just filling my belly.

Go easy on food if it's been a while since you ate, he told us. *Otherwise you'll make yourself sick, and that's something you want to avoid at all costs.*

Sergeant Bale's advice has to go through my head several times before I can make myself stop eating. Instead, I start filling Alivarda's pockets with fruit.

When I get rescued, everyone will have questions about the loss of the *Burying Ground*. The newspapers, sure, but also Parliament. That means I'll have to remember it. The way the sky darkened. The way the deck splintered beneath us.

"I don't see how I can tell the truth," I say to my dad and my heavy pockets. "That the storm hit before the treaty could be signed. This was going to be it. We won the war. The boys would come home. No more war work for kids. No more casualty lists in the newspapers. No more rationing or travel restrictions. Things were going to be *different*."

The jungle whirs and rustles around me, and dimly I can hear the muffled *crush-rush* of the ocean.

The Ariminthians mistrusted the cease-fire from the start. Their envoys kept saying *we* were the ones who didn't want peace. That all our talk of a treaty was just an excuse to draw out their king so we could assassinate him. They would not shut up about a sustained campaign of sabotage carried out by spies and terrorists when that sort of thing is completely prohibited by the Raritan Accords.

"Or," I say quietly, "I could just say the treaty *was* signed. There's no way it survived the storm, so it's not like anyone will find it and prove me wrong. I'd be the one who brought peace to Dura after all this time."

And then there *would* be parades. I'd be the guest of honor at state dinners, and people would come up to me and shake my hand and ask how it felt to be there when it happened, when the king and the prime minister each stood at that table we'd commissioned special for the occasion, the airy wrought-iron one with narrow spikes at the base of the legs so it could be secured to the deck.

All I have to do now is survive, and now that I have clothing and food, already things are better than they were an hour ago.

I can totally do this.

THEY TOLD US to expect a lot of shit work when we joined covert ops, but I had no idea that the shittiest part would be the frigging paperwork.

I roll a tiny, delicate sheet of dissolvable paper into the palm-size encryption dealie and scowl at it. This stuff is the worst. It leaves a faint slick of oil all over your hands.

Best get it over with. I groan, but softly, and start typing with the stylus. The machine changes every letter into code as I go.

Chess team reporting. Surveillance of the palace suggests they still anticipate the return of the Burying Ground. *No mourning crepe on the battlements. No unusual fleet movement.*

"Maybe if you clods would authorize, you know, *infiltration*, we might learn something actionable," I mutter, but I don't type it. I don't need another lecture about how dissolvable paper is expensive, there's a cease-fire in effect, and having opinions is for people well above my pay grade.

Besides, Command has enough on its plate now that Parliament can't pull its head out of its ass long enough to decide what pastries to serve at the emergency committee meetings, much less what to make of the *Burying Ground*'s very suspicious lateness returning to the neutral port. The opposition whip is adamant that he's still running the government and giving orders—both parties agreed to temporary powers before the sailing—but the prime minister's party wants to declare him dead so there can be a special election.

Hard to declare someone dead when there's no evidence for it. The *Burying Ground* could just be blown off course. It could have turned into a party ship, celebrating peace with high-dollar booze and taking its sweet time coming back. The Ariminthians believe it's still out there, and they're in a much better position to know.

Not that we can trust them. But still. If we're the ones to violate the cease-fire and the *Burying Ground* arrives tomorrow with that signed treaty, those antiwar clowns will have a field day.

The tiny paper is only half-full. I know I'm supposed to stick to the facts of the mission when I write these reports, but I'm not getting called on the carpet again over wasting this greasy crap.

The admiralty here has received no reports of piracy since the cease-fire. We have confirmed this through multiple sources. Known pirate vessels have moved away from shipping lanes and mining outposts. Also nowhere near where the Burying Ground *should be. Surveillance recommended.*

There.

I spin the rollers, and the encryption machine obediently spits out my report. I pull a missive container from my pocket. It's a watertight metal tube about the size of a cigarette. You can't get this paper wet until you're ready to get rid of the message. It falls apart in an oily mess if you even *think* about water.

VIVIENNE

THE SHRINE IS as lovely as I can make it. The stones are gleaming white and covered with fresh flowers. I have nothing that was hers, so there is no way to call her here, but perhaps she will come anyway.

If she comes, if she accepts the shrine as worthy, the princess will have a home in this place for always.

There will be no need for her to haunt me.

This island is ordinary, like any of the thousands settled like green jewels into the high seas. From the sand alone, I can tell there is no springwood. The war has slowed exploration and cartography to a crawl. Even the latest maps don't include every island that exists, and nothing about this place would draw a Royal Navy ship's attention.

If I'm on an island that hasn't been charted, it's all but certain I will never be found.

I will not have to return to the palace without her. I will not have to stand alone in the princess's elegant chamber with its velvet-flocked wallpaper and cozy rugs and big leaded windows. I won't have to pack my few things in a bundle, close the door one last time, and venture belowstairs to present myself to the grim, unsmiling chatelaine.

The chatelaine would know me on sight. She would remember exactly what brought me to the palace, and she would make sure I ended up in some damp, forgotten part of it now that there was no princess to do for.

But the palace is far away. Ariminthia is far away. The only thing I was there that's worth holding on to—being lady's maid to Princess Aubrielle Melisande Felicity Tiralie Vivienne of Ariminthia—I can be here.

The rest can fade into the mist, like it never was.

If the princess finds the shrine acceptable, if she comes to it, she will become a part of the island. She will convince this island to be generous and good and provide all the things I need. She will stay here with me, and I will do for her as I did in life.

I will never be alone.

The Durans may find me, though. They believe they have a right to land on any island they like and set up machines to brutally extract whatever resources exist there regardless of what is already flourishing.

Supposedly that was a key part of the treaty that the king was meant to set his seal to. The Duran government would be required to apply for permits for each colony site based on map coordinates and agree to responsible mining practices. There'd be no more fleets of greedy industrialist blackguards outfitting ships and hiring rough, feral crews with the shortsighted single-minded goal of enriching themselves, and there'd be special protections for islands where springwood grows.

Little wonder the Durans chose sabotage instead of allowing the king to seal that treaty. Anything to keep that steady march of mineral wealth into their factories.

Anything to prevent their enemy from carefully harvesting the best wood for sloops and dreadnoughts and all else that must withstand the sea.

The minister for counterterrorism nearly didn't allow the *Burying Ground* to leave the neutral port. He personally searched a Duran girl three different times, and she could not keep from rolling her eyes when he made her hand over first her powder compact and then a belt with extra buckles.

He begged the king to stay onshore. Or at the very least to insist the Duran girl's father be dismissed from the peace accords and another reporter sent in his place. One whose children were small and more likely to be harmless.

Better yet, no reporters at all. No one whose sole purpose is to sway the minds of the biddable with a version of the truth that suits the needs of industry and government.

The king would not hear of it. The Durans routinely engaged in sabotage, but a ship with their head of state on board—and his family, and the families of the top four functionaries in the republic of Dura, as well as that of a newspaperman meant to document the whole thing—that ship would surely be safe.

But a prime minister can be elected. Functionaries can be appointed. Newspapermen are no better than peasants. Royal blood comes into the world but one way, and when it's gone, it's gone forever.

The Durans had no liking for the treaty. They made no secret of that. But the Royal Navy can sink anything they put in the water, so they are not able to mass an army and invade outright.

Only if Ariminthia is torn apart by civil war could Dura come out the victor, and they are bloodthirsty and callous enough to sacrifice a few of their own to bring that about. It may be the sole advantage of the circus they call a government—everyone is expendable.

Soon Ariminthia will fall. It does not bear thinking on.

Perhaps that is what the sea intended. That the princess and I should know peace, and there will be no peace in Ariminthia once Duran boots hit the soil.

All at once I know she has found the shrine. There is something in the wink of light off the stones, the fragrance of the flowers whose scent should be fading instead of growing stronger.

It will be her and me, then. We will mourn Ariminthia, but we will no longer be bound to it.

This island is a gift. The princess hated the war, hated that we had to fight at all. All three of the royal sisters did, but my mistress had constant nightmares about it. A pirate fleet taking advantage of the navy's distraction and sacking the capital. Her fathers cut to slivers by Duran war machines and left to bleach on the sand. Her brother captured, publicly tortured, pieces of him swaying from a gibbet. None of them given to the sea in death, all of them homeless, furious, haunting her.

The princess always said she just wanted it to be over. Now it is for her. For us both.

This is a beautiful place to spend eternity.

CORA

ALL RIGHT. HERE'S what I know:

The fruit I found is tasty and edible, but it's not very filling. I'm going to have to find some sort of stick-to-your-ribs food soon, because there's a pit in my stomach that I remember from the famine year. It's a dull ache now, but it's only going to get worse.

There's a freshwater spring near my berry patch. It's clear and cold, and I may have wept actual tears when I found it. The only downside is that it's a good distance from my camp, and not fun to find at night.

When the sun goes down, there's not a mouthful of light from anywhere. The birdcalls fade, and the only sound that reminds you that you're not dead and buried is the ocean's *shush-shush*.

In the dark, you will remember when you were very small

and your parents dropped you off at nursery and you watched them walk away, and you knew they were coming back but *what if they didn't*, and that same horrible, hollow feeling opens up inside you now, and you will cry. You will pull your piece of sail-cloth tight across your shoulders as a makeshift blanket and hum a song and count the moments till the sky grows pale and a new day gives you light, and then you will feel kind of ridiculous being scared of the dark like the nursery kids you tuck in at naptime.

Another thing I know: no matter how I bash, smash, pry, or swear, the lock on that valise is not giving way. I can't even jam a stick where the two halves of this suitcase meet and force them open. Because I don't know what's in there, of course I'm imagining it's a flare gun or a ten-course steak dinner or aloe for my raw, peeling sunburn, even though it's probably someone's underwear and tooth powder.

Last thing: it's a lot harder than you'd think to make a shelter.

In invasion readiness training, Sergeant Bale spent a whole day explaining different ways to rig a makeshift shelter. *You will probably not be lucky enough to have materials with you*, he said. *It's likely if you're using this training at all, you had to flee without much time to pack. At that point, consider everything yours for the taking. It now belongs to the enemy, so there's no such thing as stealing. Your primary goal is survival.*

Your secondary goal is sabotage.

There we were, twelve years old, some wide-eyed, others

hard and steely, awaiting our first war work assignments and learning what to do if the Ariminthians invaded Dura. We cut limbs from big dry pines and laid them slantwise against fallen logs. We pegged sheets of canvas to the ground in windswept fields and held them up in the middle with branches or broomsticks. That show-off Kess stole a bedsheet from a washing line and everyone expected her to get chewed out by Sergeant Bale, but instead he awarded her a pocket compass as a prize for *using what the land gave her.*

At the end of the day, though, we'd be home. Sitting at the dinner table with our parents. Tending our victory gardens and knitting scarves for soldiers. Inside four walls we didn't have to build ourselves.

I still haven't found any sign of my mom and dad.

Stay busy, Sergeant Bale told us. *Don't let yourself start thinking about the situation you're in. Otherwise you'll make bad decisions. Stay busy, stay alert, and stay focused on your primary goal.*

"All right," I tell him, although I'm not sure how I'm supposed to *forget* I've been shipwrecked in pirate-infested waters and possibly orphaned, but whatever. Staying busy is not the worst idea, and I really don't want to spend another night without some kind of roof over my head.

Use what the land gives you, said Sergeant Bale, and the jungle next to the beach is giving me long, ropy vines made of some kind of stringy stem, like giant leggy dandelions without the yellow flower. They braid real nice, and after a while—probably hours, maybe days, but it's a task and I focus—I have enough braided vine rope to suspend my piece of sailcloth at an angle on the edge of the beach.

I stand back and admire it. It's like half a tent, minus two sides and a front.

"There," I tell Sergeant Bale. "Off the sand because of the fleas, eww, but close enough in case a ship passes by. If someone aboard sees a shelter, they're going to be curious."

These islands are too far away from anything to be inhabited—which is why these waters were chosen for the treaty signing—and none of them are big enough to support a population anyway. A visible shack gets me rescued.

Then I have a thought.

The ship will probably be Ariminthian.

We have a few ships that can handle long voyages on the high seas, but mostly it's Ariminthian vessels that sail around out here.

They might kill me on sight. The whole reason we're at war is their brutal, unprovoked attacks on Duran mining camps on uninhabited islands like this one, and the fact that there's a cease-fire in effect and also that I'm a girl may not matter to them.

I'm not sure I like my other option, though. The one that involves waiting till Dura lurches a ship all the way out to wherever this place is.

I'm thinking about the situation I'm in, like I'm not supposed to. At least I have shelter now. Maybe the dark won't be so scary tonight.

"You know what would make it even less scary?" I ask my tent. "A fire. Right here in front of you. Nice and cozy. Keep any big jungle animals away, too."

Make sure your wood is completely dry, Sergeant Bale told us, *or it'll send up a plume of smoke that'll be like a finger pointing down from the heavens directly at you.*

Oh.

Invasion readiness training was all about learning to stay hidden so you could stay alive. Right now I need to be the opposite of hidden.

A giant bonfire in the middle of the beach crammed with green palm branches just might be the saving of me.

I hurry to the nearest palm that's short enough for me to reach its fronds. Alivarda's jackknife blade is tiny, but I grab hold of a branch and start sawing where it meets the scaly trunk.

The bark is like leather. It does *not* want to be cut, and once it is, the inside is wet and pulpy and even harder to cut.

I grit my teeth, wipe plant juice on Alivarda's trousers, and keep sawing away.

I only have a handful of fronds when I lose patience, grab one in each hand, and tow them toward the beach. The fronds are heavier than they look. They catch the undergrowth and snag on brush. I swear loudly—no one's here to tell me to watch my language—and I'm breathing hard by the time I yank them onto the sand, where they glide.

It's a task and I focus. I cut and drag fronds till the pile is big enough to get a fire started, and I'm a sweaty mess. I lean half a dozen boughs into a sagging pyramid, arrange some tinder in the middle, and search the beach till I find a little piece of flint. There are a bunch washed up amid the driftwood, winking black here and there like insects. I scrape Alivarda's little knife down the flint till sparks jump out in sheets, then crouch beside the tiny embers and blow, gentle and patient like Sergeant Bale showed us.

Before long the fire catches, and soon flames creep up and through the boughs. The smoke is a wisp at first, but soon it's pushing up in huge bulbous puffs and, boy, does it *reek*.

I'm sure not going to be afraid of the dark tonight, but this smell is *never* coming out of my hair.

"All right," I say to the fire. "You are looking healthy and excellent. Now I just have to keep you burning till a ship spots your smoke. Then I'll get rescued and go home."

Just the thought of walking through my front door without my mom and dad hits me square like a punch to the guts. Everything will be as we left it. The throw blanket draped over the reading chair. The wood floors polished to a shine. The door to their room pulled closed to keep in the heat.

Or maybe they'll be aboard the rescue ship. Or on the other side of the island. Or back in Dura already, talking to reporters before I get the chance to.

I'm thinking about my situation again.

I sink down in a patch of shade, empty the waterskin—*stay hydrated, even though it means you'll need to pee*—and watch my fire proudly. Keeping it burning is going to take a lot of palm fronds, and cutting them with a silly little jackknife is going to keep me busy, all right.

If someone was going to sneak a weapon on board, wouldn't they go for something more, I don't know, *violent*? One that wasn't the length of my finger and full of rope strands and tucked away in a sea bag?

Then I giggle, helplessly, because an Ariminthian breaking the rules might just be the thing that saves my life.

VIVIENNE

THE ISLAND HAS offered some branches that I turn into an arbor, and now there is shade beside the shrine. The island has shown me where to find berries and fresh water, and my belly is full of sweet fruit.

The princess is content. I have done right by her, and we are at peace here, together.

I sit near the shrine in the warm sand and admire the sky. It's an endless wash of blue, and the ocean swishes busily ashore. Farther out, there's a misty bar where sea and sky fold together somehow, where there is nothing and no one.

Only . . . there is something. A dark object bobbing at some distance. Not moving on its own, and not any shape that might be alive.

It has the lines and corners of an Ariminthian sea chest.

My mistress is more than content. She is delighted. It would have been enough with just the island providing, but now the sea shares gifts as well.

I murmur my thanks, then pull my shift over my head and toss it onto the sand before wading into the surf.

I stop knee-deep, the tide pulling at my bare shins. Just like it did when I was small and I held tight to my father's fingers as the waves in the harbor bumped my chubby baby legs. The smell of brine rises sharp, and my father is laughing because I'm crouching down, trying to hug each wave as it hits my chest, me squealing and splashing and digging my toes in the sand.

Mama told me to forget about him. Perhaps then everyone else would, too.

I did. I had.

But I am remembering now, trailing my fingertips through the water, how my father waded into the sea and held open his arms for me to swim to. Farther and farther out he went, till I had no need to touch the bottom to feel safe.

I am remembering how gendarmes in royal livery hauled my father away, his big hobnail boots leaving wet saltwater streaks on the weathered timber of the docks.

Lèse majesté, their captain told my trembling mother as she clutched her sewing with both hands. *Insulting the dignity of the Crown.*

I wade out farther. The water is dishpan warm and gently rolling. The princess barely tolerated bathing and preferred to appreciate the sea through the window, which made letting go of those long afternoons in the harbor that much easier.

I pull in a swim breath and dive. My body remembers how to kick and glide. Even the choppy ocean doesn't slow me down, and soon I'm treading water next to the sea chest. It dips and sways, and I have no trouble nudging it in front of me till I reach the shallows.

Once the trunk is beached, I undo the series of latches. Inside the chest are rows and rows of sea rations—dried meat, hardtack, and bags of slightly withered limes, all packed tight in oilcloth. There's a hint of mustiness, but this chest was made with sturdy oak and painted inside and out with tar. Springwood is precious enough to be reserved for ships, but oak can take tough storms and keep provisions dry and edible.

I shift the rations in batches up to the princess's shrine. I put shavings of the meat and a squeeze of lime into scalloped shells by her grave, and I thank her and the island and the sea for making sure I would eat well.

Once the trunk is empty, I put my shoulder against it and push it toward her shrine. It leaves thick grooves in the sand. I'm not sure what the princess means for me to do with it, but she sent it to me and I won't insult her by rejecting a gift.

It's not big enough to sleep in, but when I tip it on its side, it makes a nice windbreak. I shift and shuffle it so it's at an angle with her shrine. My mistress will like seeing it. She will like knowing it's here.

Now that I know to look to the sea for provisions, I move

down to the waterline and really look. Several more shapes are visible in the distance, and in a few swims, I have enough sea rations to last for months, as well as small helpful things like clothing and cutlery and sewing kits and twine.

I arrange everything so the princess can see it. Once that's done, I go to the waterline one last time, just to make sure I didn't miss anything she sent.

That's when I see the smoke.

It rises sheer and black from a part of the island some distance away, blotting out the sky in a column before drifting into an angry blight of haze.

It's too precise to be natural. It's how smoke looks when it stems from an act of violence.

No. The war is far away. It would not know to find us here.

The princess must want me to see this. Something is not right, and she would have me find out what it is.

I put my dress back on and set off along the waterline, keeping that pillar of smoke in front of me. I don't think too much about *where*. Instead I picture the princess in her room. Sitting on that low stool with the blue cushion, facing away. She has a party to go to, and I'm to arrange her hair.

My mistress went to a lot of parties, mostly because her sisters felt sorry for her and insisted she be included. The two elder princesses were a year apart and liked the same music, the same activities, the same foods. The same boys, sometimes. My mistress was five years behind the younger one. The youngest of the royal children.

The afterthought, she would mutter, despite all the complicated and very public family planning.

Her sisters spent every party and function drifting gracefully through well-heeled crowds, charming noble lords and royal officials with their warmth and good cheer. My mistress could barely carry on a conversation, chewing her fingernails to pulp and stumbling over every other word, especially in a hall full of music and chatter and swirling dresses and bumping elbows and strangers she was supposed to remember.

My mistress did what she could to avoid these events, but her sisters would have none of it. If one of them got an invitation to a dance or a dinner, all of them would go or none of them would.

I was the one who suggested that sometimes she could just be ill. Not every time, not twice in a row. But sometimes. Those days when you were made of emptiness and yet your limbs were too heavy to shift out of bed. Those days when thinking any thought was like wading through wet gray mush.

The princess looked at me like I was a towering genius instead of a girl who peeled turnips all day, who still cried herself to sleep every night because she missed that little shack on the wharf-side and the *pop* of her mother's sewing needle going through canvas and the smell of her father's dockworker greatcoat—brine and tar and the chilly fog off the harbor.

After that, I did not go back to peeling turnips. Instead I took up residence on that little pallet at the foot of her bed. I began to mend dresses and keep secrets.

The smell of smoke is oppressive now, and even though it stinks, it's not the reek of charred concrete and burning flesh. It does not smell of war and sabotage and terror.

I round a headland and stagger to a stop.

There on the beach is a massive pyre of palm fronds. Smoke pours upward, fouling the endless blue.

This is not a fire for cooking. This is not a fire to keep a room warm.

This must be a clear-cut fire. The kind set by Durans to destroy springwood trees so they can more easily gut the earth below.

My breath comes out in shudders even as I realize I'm wrong. The fire is on the beach by itself. Not raging freely through the jungle, leaving everything a smoking ruin.

Still, I cannot ignore that the princess sent me here. Perhaps she cannot bear the smell of fire. Perhaps it's too close to war.

I find a piece of driftwood still soaked from its time in the sea. I wedge it into the bottom of the pyre and scatter those burning fronds every which way. I kick sand on each one till they're not even smoldering, then I spit on the lot.

Near the tree line, all but hidden from sight, there is a pitiful shelter made of canvas held up with strands of tortured vines. It has Duran fingerprints all over it. The cutting of healthy fronds. The harsh, casual destruction of the natural world for personal gain.

I storm over to it, and I'm about to tear it down when I spot the sea bag.

I am remembering how my mother would sew bags like this one by the window where the light was best, how an agent from the palace would come once a month to collect them, how she would receive a benediction if she'd produced more than was required.

I am remembering going down to the admiralty dockyard to watch the palace agent give the bags to new sailors and marines, how they didn't look much older than me, how I wished they knew how many prayers for their safety my mother had put into her stitching.

I am remembering the faces of these boys as they did their duty at their lords' command, how they gripped those bags as if they knew they would need all the prayers they could get.

The sea is strange, but I cannot think of a single reason why it would deliver an Ariminthian sea bag to a Duran.

Yet it has.

The princess and the island are one now. There's absolutely no reason under the depthless and unforgiving sea that she would allow the enemy to share it with us.

I pick up the empty sea bag and run my fingers over the complex stitching.

There's a shuffle in the thick stand of trees where the sand peters out, and a girl appears.

She's moving ponderously, towing half a dozen large palm fronds with a complicated harness that she has crafted from a length of ratline. When she sees me, she stops in a skid of sand

and squawks something in Duran, a surprised yelp like a dog when you step on its tail.

I back up a pace, then another, holding the sea bag tight over my heart.

No. This is not right. This is *not right*.

The Duran girl is still talking, a babble of words pouring from her like a baby's nonsense prattle, but I am realizing why my mistress led me here, over the sand, with smoke of all things.

This invader has little food and water in her camp. The sea will not deliver rations to her. Her shelter won't stand up to weather, and she is thin and hollow at the eyes like a scullery servant trying to survive on turnip peels.

The princess wanted me to see what she and the island have in store for anyone who dares disrupt our sanctuary.

The island will end the Duran girl in its own time. She will wither like a springwood tree that struggles to grow in soil whose mineral content has been extracted.

There is no need for war when the princess has decided that there will be peace here, in this place, whether the invader likes it or not.

The Duran girl is still talking, struggling to free herself from that ridiculous harness, when I turn on my heel and walk away, the sea bag over my shoulder where it belongs.

AFTER I SENT that report about the pirate fleet, I kicked myself. Rook and King may have kicked me a few times, too. I know better than to include *surveillance recommended* in a report. It pretty much guarantees that your team will be the one assigned to said surveillance.

Surveillance is downright boring when you're used to *real* war work, and I honestly cannot see why the pirates should be our problem when we're all bracing for news of the *Burying Ground*.

Still, orders are orders. Command knows what it's doing.

Chess team reporting. Pirate movement remains negligible. The admiralty has received no reports of vessel seizures since the cease-fire. Last confirmed pirate action was the looting of the Mariner's Glory, *three days before the news went public. Butcher's bill was twenty hands lost along with a cargo of grain.*

I'm not sure what else Command would find useful. I'm not supposed to speculate, but there's only so much we can learn onshore. Pirate fleets operate out on the high seas, sinking troop ships and burning outposts and basically giving the finger to Parliament every chance they get.

If you believe the Ariminthians, the pirates are making their lives hard as well. They swear up and down that the Royal Navy bust their asses trying to eliminate the pirate problem. That's been the official word out of the admiralty ever since Parliament accused them of manning the pirate ships themselves, or at least funding and outfitting them while turning a blind eye, but it's also what the chatter on the docks says, so maybe it's true. Pretty much every ship that the pirates use was built in Ariminthia, but that's probably because theirs are better than ours by orders of magnitude. If you're going to steal something and use it to shut down shipping lanes and send cannon to the bottom, you might as well go first cabin.

The pirates seem like they're everywhere, especially in the last six months. There's more and more chaos and violence on the high seas, which means more shortages, which means more antiwar demonstrations by those doorknobs in Embrace Piss, to the point where Parliament has had to whomp up a new act to deal with their unpatriotic nonsense. Command works pretty hard to keep us in the dark when it comes to stuff like that—*mission-focused*, they like to say—but there's usually a way to find things out.

The mood of the docks is tense. Folks are concerned for the royal family's well-being, but also the treaty and whether there's peace.

For all the stupid crap that monarchies do, the Ariminthians have the right idea when it comes to treason—lock that shit down hard with a horror-show punishment. They don't even dress it up in pretty language. Parliament's Defense of Liberty Emergency Powers Act should be called the Shut Up, Traitors Act, and it should do a hell of a lot more than curtail what you can say in public and what you can print in a newspaper.

I tap the stylus against my chin. There's something else. Something weird.

The counterterrorism minister arrived in the royal carriage when he turned up for his weekly meeting at the admiralty yesterday.

Guy's name is Ingannaro, and he might be the most important person in the realm outside the royal family, but he's still outside the royal family. He has no business in that carriage.

If there was literally *any* other indication that the palace considered the *Burying Ground* lost—the Royal Mother's barge arriving, space being cleared in the city for one of those stupid shrines, the king's brothers returning from the front—this would be extremely significant.

There's still a strip of space at the bottom of the report. We've been told to surveil the docks and find out what we can about pirates. The counterterrorism minister is not a pirate, and I absolutely *do not* need another ass-chewing about my reports.

I spin the wheels of the encryption device, roll up my report, then go wash the grease from the paper off my hands.

VIVIENNE

THE SHRINE TAKES up most of my days. Every morning, it must be swept clean of blown sand. I rub the white stones with wax from the small pot that on shipboard would serve the astrolabe and compass. Then I gather flowers, fresh and at the peak of bloom, and lay them like a coverlet over those stones.

I'm placing the last blossom when someone clears their throat. I startle and scramble, and when I turn, there she is. The Duran girl. She's standing a distance away, on the beach, holding out both hands palms up. This is supposedly a Duran way to tell someone they are unarmed, but I don't believe it for a moment.

She's wearing a shirt and trousers that don't belong to her.

"Hello," she says in the common language, but then she pauses, like she'd planned to say something else but now she's not sure it's right.

I move several steps forward, big steps, so she won't come closer. So she'll look at me, not the shrine.

The Duran girl backs away a pace, but only a pace. Then she holds her ground.

"Wow. Okay. So there really is another person here." She toes the sand. "I guess I kind of freaked out when I saw you. No wonder you took off."

I haven't spoken the common language in years. Not since my father was arrested for lèse majesté and sentenced to die and our family fined a thousand gold thalers.

"I'm Cora," she says, and her voice is growing less steady. "What are you called?"

Not since my mother wept at the servants' entrance to the palace and gave me over to the chatelaine so I could spend the rest of my life in remunerative servitude, working off that unfathomable and purposefully crushing debt.

I am remembering, and I would not be remembering had this Duran girl not appeared. I would be thinking about the princess and tending her shrine and allowing the island to do away with the menace however it saw fit.

"Ah. All right. You don't have to tell me that." The girl takes in my camp with a slight frown. "Are you here by yourself? I was hoping there were others. Have you seen anyone else?"

"You—you are not welcome here." I stumble over the common language like a toddler. "How did you find this place?"

She gestures toward the beach. "The tracks. You walked here over the sand, above the tide line. I followed your trail."

I dig my fingernails into my skin hard enough to sting. That was foolish. *I* was foolish. All I had to do was return through the shallows and there'd be a good chance she never would have found me. Now she is here, and she knows I'm alone.

I thought the island was taking care of this sort of thing.

"I was . . ." The girl looks down. "I thought my parents could be on the island, too. They were on the ship with us. Redheaded, both of them. I thought maybe you'd seen them?"

"The ship," I repeat, and I am living it again, choking on salt water, fighting for breath, watching her die.

Ending up here.

Standing face-to-face with the girl that the minister for counterterrorism personally searched three times. The one most likely to have sent that ship to the bottom.

The Duran girl looks even worse up close. Her skin is sunburned and peeling, her eyes sunk deep into her face.

Perhaps she meant to go down with the *Burying Ground*. Perhaps she never thought she'd survive the sabotage meant to end the war the only way the Durans ever could.

"I've seen no one else," I reply, and when her shoulders slump, I come close to pitying her.

Neither of us speak. The seabirds screech and wing above us. The sea turns and tumbles, then slithers up the shore. The tide is coming in.

I think she might be crying.

"Well." The girl drags a dirty cuff over her eyes, pulls herself together, and grits a smile. "That just leaves you and me, then. Guess that means you're the one who wrecked my signal fire. Right? Did you not know what it was for?"

I go cold all over. The last thing I want is to leave this island. The princess is here. The war is not. The island will provide everything I need to serve her here, where both of us are safe and content.

The girl is still talking. ". . . thought it would make sense to share a single camp. Especially if it's true that we're the only ones here, and who knows what kinds of dangerous animals live in that jungle?"

No dangerous animals live in that jungle, which she would know if Durans spent half a moment investigating and researching things instead of actively destroying them.

"Besides, it's not just animals we should be worried about," she adds, filling the spaces where I am not putting words. "There's pirates, too."

If the sea means to take you, there will be a long pull of salty water and a moment of panic and then—peace. Pirates leave few survivors and fewer corpses. It's not difficult to determine the reason.

"See?" The girl edges a step closer. Her voice seems bright and friendly, as if I'd just let slip a secret. "You're worried about pirates, too. We stand a better chance of being rescued if we . . ."

She trails off, sifting for the right words. She can't even say *work together.* I fold my arms tighter and watch her squirm through a transparently false attempt at courtesy.

This girl thinks to be rescued. She could unwittingly summon pirates instead. Or perhaps that's her plan. Pirates are Duran to a man, and once she told them she was a survivor of the *Burying Ground,* they'd realize she was worth a ransom. They'd bring her on shipboard and cut my throat.

Once they were done with me.

The island would never allow it. Neither would the sea. The princess will whisper in the island's ear and it will stir the sea, and together they will protect me from both rescue and pirates.

There's nothing this Duran girl can do against the combined force of the island and the sea. She can light ten thousand fires. She can scream into the wind. She will slowly starve here, blistered by the sun, and the island will make sand of her bones.

"You have brought the war here," I tell her, "so you are not welcome. There will be no rescue. Please leave and don't come back."

The girl looks lost, standing there bedraggled and alone. I'm glad I have the princess for company, or else I might feel as bad as she looks.

Finally she turns. She walks a dozen paces down the beach, then looks back. When I don't move, she pivots and keeps walking until sand and sky swallow her up.

CORA

"ALL RIGHT, SO *that* was a mistake," I say to Sergeant Bale as I shush through the shallows of the ocean, up to my ankles in soothing warm water. "I know. I know. I broke every rule you tried to teach me. I told her my name. My *real* name. I said I was alone. And I . . . well . . ."

I showed weakness in front of the enemy. Even if she's a girl who can barely put a sentence together. Because I got scared.

Because I was stupid enough to believe we had one simple thing in common.

All at once I remember her from the *Burying Ground*. She spent most of her time standing behind the youngest princess, the one who was too high-and-mighty to even nod politely when my parents greeted her. Oh, no. Her Royal Snideness kept her eyes on her expensive-looking leather boots and snubbed them.

We learned in school that most Ariminthians are servants or

peasants. They don't have a choice, and even if they did, they'd choose to stay servants because they've been kept ignorant on purpose and don't know better.

War work may not be glamorous, and everyone over twelve might have to do it, but at least I'm not a servant.

I wonder if she means it. That she's not interested in being rescued.

Oh.

Perhaps it's not that she doesn't want to leave. It's that she thinks to escape on her own and abandon me here to rot. I had to walk quite a ways to get to her camp. A ship could anchor off that side of the island and I'd never see it.

"But you know what?" I go on, and now I'm talking to my feet in the surf, the foam skidding up so pretty on the sand. "I'm done thinking about her. I don't need her to get off this island. She's been taught to braid hair. I know how to purify water with a sun still. I'll be the one leaving *her* to rot."

The last thing we had to do in invasion readiness training was the wilderness drop. On a random morning, unknown to us but agreed to by our parents, we were pulled out of bed before dawn, bundled into the back of a wagon, blindfolded, and left alone one by one in the middle of nowhere, each with nothing but a bottle of water, a first-aid kit, and a sharp knife. We were to make our way home however we could, using the skills we'd been taught, and there was a ribbon and bragging rights for the best time.

It's a wonder that Ariminthian girl has stayed alive as long as she has on this island, given how little she must know.

Back in camp, I sit on my rock and scowl at my blisters and think about how much work it's going to be to build another fire.

You have brought the war here.

"I'm not the one who ruined a perfectly good signal fire," I tell her. "I'm going to have to watch the next one, too, so you don't trash it again."

I'm going to have to decide what I'll do if I catch her in the act.

I eat a few handfuls of daleberries, but I'm still hungry and it's a swirly, light-headed kind of hungry. I've felt like this before, the famine year, and I know exactly what I need: protein.

That'll be tomorrow's task. Make a trap and catch a bird before I get too addled and staggery from hunger.

"But what if I can't?" I ask the bare stretch of sand and the leather valise I still can't open.

The Ariminthian girl didn't look like she was surviving on daleberries. She looked better than healthy. She must be catching birds in the jungle or fish in the ocean, and if she can do it, it must be way easy.

Now I'm thinking about eating birds and fish, and it makes me smile. We hardly ever have meat at home because of rationing, but I'll build another fire and figure out how to cook something once I catch it. It'll be *easy*.

———

THE FIRE IS easy. The trap is hard.

While the signal blaze sends up its column of smoke, I spend days trying to tie vines and sticks into a cage, but the result is falling-apart ridiculous.

At least I'm not thinking about the situation I'm in. I'm too busy weaving vines into a truly garbage excuse for a net that might catch the world's stupidest fish if I'm lucky.

When the net is done—or at least not actively falling apart—I walk up the beach and around the headland to a place where the water goes deep all of a sudden. I know basically nothing about fish, but it seems like a place they might like to swim around.

The water glints in bright jags. I look up and away and—

Something has edged around the far end of the island, dark against the smudgy blue expanse of ocean. I have to look and look again before my brain lets me believe my eyes.

It's a ship.

Somehow my fire must have worked.

It is a ship and I am *saved*.

VIVIENNE

THE SEA IS strange. This is something everyone knows. The sea must be flattered, feted, courted, loved.

It's best to stay in the sea's good graces, but sometimes it will do a thing that is purely unknowable, just to remind you that it can.

This is the only way I'm able to account for the ship that nudges past a long sandy spit and into view.

This is not how I thought the island would rid itself of the Duran girl, but at least she will be gone. She will get on that ship and take the war home with her, where it cannot harm us. This island will belong to my mistress once again. It will be ours to share.

Unless the Duran girl says something to the captain about me.

My heart starts hurting in big, deep throbs.

She wouldn't even have to mean any harm. All she must do is be honest when he'll inevitably ask whether anyone else is on the island. Durans are inveterate liars, but perhaps she'll think of it as a kindness. A gesture of peace in the spirit of the cease-fire.

I have to get to the Duran girl before the ship's boat lands. She can't tell them I'm here. No captain, Duran or Ariminthian or pirate, would let any survivor of the *Burying Ground* remain.

I round the headland and spot her on the beach next to a pile of palm fronds and another fire belching out smoke. She's down by the waterline waving a piece of sailcloth, trying to get the ship's attention.

I'm running over the sand. Stumbling when my ankles sink. She must hear me coming because she turns, grinning so big and open that for a moment I'm shaken. She looks like an ordinary girl. A daughter of the gentry or some noble lord. Someone who'd be at one of the princess's dances or singing in the drawing room to the *plinkity-plink* of the pianoforte.

"Look!" she squeals in the common language. "We're saved!"

"I don't want to be rescued." It comes out blunt. "Tell them nothing about me."

Her lips flap until she manages, *"What?"*

"You heard what I said."

The Duran girl nods slowly. "You're mad. But whatever. Rot here if that's what you want."

What I want. It stills me. It has been many long years since

I've done something merely because I want to.

I am turning to leave, to disappear myself into the jungle where the vessel will not mark me, but something about the ship makes me look at it again. It's a brigantine, rigged for patrol, perhaps eight guns and—

It's not flying any colors.

I hadn't noticed at a distance, but now that I'm closer, I can't take my eyes off the bare aftermast. The blatant disregard for maritime custom and seagoing law. Even Durans fly their insignia on their pitiful fleet of barges and tubs.

This is a pirate vessel. And that Duran girl is busily waving them down.

"Stop! Right now! This is bad!" I'm still stumbling over the common language. When she turns to me, incredulous, I struggle for the right words. "Why do you bring them here?"

"To rescue us, of course!" the Duran girl replies. "Those have to be your people, looking for survivors of the *Burying Ground*. That's me. You can do what you want, but I mean to go with them."

When I don't reply, she peers at me. "Aren't they? You aren't—what's going on here?"

A ship's boat is being lowered over the side of the pirate vessel, and distant shapes are climbing in one by one.

"Wait. Wait. They're not in uniform." The Duran girl's eyes grow large. "Oh crackers. They're pirates!"

She races past me, up the beach and into her camp. "This is bad. We're dead. We are *worse* than dead."

"But this is good news for you," I reply bitterly, following her. "Pirates are all Duran. They will take you home."

"*What?*" Her voice goes high and angry. "It's *your* filthy lot who are pirates!"

"That is—that is lies."

"Whatever. Get out of my way." The girl shoves me aside and grabs things from around her camp. Things that don't belong to her, that she has clearly stolen from the island, and therefore the princess. There's a length of ratline coiled over her shoulder and a leather waterskin in her hand. But when she picks up the royal penner, I choke on a cry.

I've seen that black case only a handful of times in my years at the palace. Inside is the royal seal of Ariminthia. Had that day on the *Burying Ground* gone differently, the king would have sat at that wrought-iron table across from the Duran prime minister and four of their functionaries. He would have opened this case, run a stick of crimson wax through a candle, dripped some on that treaty, and pressed this heavy metal insignia against the molten puddle.

The war would have ended.

Peace is the last thing the Durans wanted. But the sea has other ideas.

The royal family kept a very careful muzzle on the news that it shared with the realm. There were things that the people couldn't be told, because then it was only a matter of time before the enemy learned of them.

So only a handful of people know that two of the king's

three brothers are dead. The other is missing and presumed captured, which is the same as being dead, because the Durans will deny they ever had him and have likely long since disposed of the body with quicklime and a very deep hole.

Now that the *Burying Ground* has gone down, there is no direct heir to the throne. The advisory council will have to tell the realm what has befallen the king's brothers. They will have to admit that they've known for a long time. They will try to choose who is best suited to rule, but there is little chance the noble lords will agree without a fight. There are a handful of these lords with a teaspoon of royal blood—an ancestor born on the wrong side of the blankets—but that's barely a claim, and each is bloodthirsty enough to plunge the realm into civil war before acknowledging another of their number as king.

Unless there is someone else. Someone those ruthless tooth-and-nail lords would be reluctant to array themselves against, especially after the loss of the *Burying Ground*. Someone enough of those men might line up behind if it meant they could save face.

Someone like the Royal Mother.

She does not have a claim to the throne, not like the baseborn lords, and she has not been trained in statecraft. She gave birth to four healthy children who everyone loves, and now she spends her days however she likes, which is painting in watercolors and riding her horse.

The Royal Mother cannot take the throne, but she could be made regent. The advisory council could help her learn to govern. And if she had the royal seal, it would be very difficult for the noble lords to stand against her and the advisory council to refuse her.

The sea sent the royal seal here, to this island where I washed up and built a shrine and made a home for the princess. Little wonder she was drawn here. She hated the war, and civil war would be even worse.

My mistress means for the Royal Mother to have the seal. She would have her mother become the regent of Ariminthia.

The Duran girl is struggling to hold on to all of her stolen things, the rope sliding off her shoulder and the waterskin fumbly in her hand. She cannot take her eyes off the pirates bobbing nearer every moment.

"Let me carry something," I say. "You'll be able to run faster."

The girl peers at me, half-surprised and half-suspicious. "All right. But I know where your camp is. Don't think you can just keep whatever I give you."

I reach casually for the penner dangling from her hand, but she bundles the coil of ratline into my arms instead. I try not to let my disappointment show, but I must fail because she grins in the most insolent way.

"Go now," she whispers, "but don't run. You'll draw their attention."

Every part of me wants to rush to the princess, to defend her against the pirates if it comes to that, but her shrine is far enough up the beach that it's easy to miss.

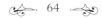

She would have me recover the seal from the Duran girl. By wit if possible. By force if necessary.

The Duran girl is already moving into the jungle, quick and silent.

"Can't we—" I choke on it. "Can't we stay together?"

A look of contempt flashes across her face, but before I can get angry, she grabs my arm and pulls me after her.

CORA

I BROUGHT PIRATES here. Me. I did that. I did not stop to think for *one second* that someone would come who would want to skin me for fun and profit instead of bringing me home to a hero's welcome.

"Stupid, stupid," I mutter, and this time I'm talking to no one but myself.

I can't keep messing up like this. There's a reason kids are sent to invasion readiness training. Sergeant Bale's only job was to see that each of us had some basic skills that would keep us alive in situations precisely like this.

I just wish he'd told us how it would feel. Being hunted. How hard it would be to stay steady. To focus.

My first priority is survival. Pirates want loot. That's what all the papers say. Food and liquor and captives. Weapons and stores meant for the boys overseas. Ore destined for Duran smithies. Fruit to feed kids in nurseries. Eat it, use it, dump it, set it on fire just to watch it burn. Worse things the papers can't print but certainly hint at.

The pirates saw me on the beach. Now I am loot.

I'm making every step count, like Sergeant Bale showed us, but it's hard because I'm also freaking out. The Ariminthian girl crashes along behind me, snapping branches and crunching leaves like some kind of animal.

"Will you hush?" I hiss, glaring over my shoulder.

For a moment she looks baffled, then she looks pained, but she at least seems to try as she follows after.

The jungle sounds take over, *whirrrrrrrrrr-cheecheechee*, but it doesn't drown out her complete inability to move quietly. The pirates are going to hear us. They're going to follow the sounds, and they're going to find us. Two girls with one flimsy jackknife between them.

"You've been trained for this," I remind myself in a ragged whisper. "What would Sergeant Bale say?"

The enemy will have the advantage of numbers. Give them as little to work with as you can.

Use what the land gives you.

At this point, there's no shame in anything you do.

We're a good distance from where we started, so I stop and turn in a slow circle where I stand. The ground is scattered with low brush, daleberry bushes mostly, and the damp, rotting remains of fallen trees and branches all being reclaimed by moss. The canopy above us is dense and lush, allowing dapples of only the most determined sunlight and thin whispers of blue sky. I put one hand on the twisted, knobby bark of a big tree, then look up about fifteen feet to where the lowest branch juts out.

"Hey." I turn to the Ariminthian girl. "Can you climb a tree?"

She looks as if I asked if she could turn dog doo into gold.

"Whatever. Good luck with the pirates." I pull my rope out of her hands, thread one end through the handle of the valise, and secure the case to my back. When I grab my first handholds in the bark's deep grooves, she grips my sleeve.

"If you leave me to them, I'll tell them where you're hiding." Her eyes are that pale Ariminthian blue, washed out like an old bedsheet. "If I die, you die, too."

Typical. I shift the weight on my back and glare at her. "There's nothing to hide behind down here on the ground, so the best chance of escaping their notice is in the canopy up there. Let me ask again: can you climb a tree?"

She looks down and shakes her head once, sharp and final.

Crackers, how could these people have ever fought us to a standstill? "Can you at least climb a rope?"

I expect another helpless, useless refusal to so much as meet me halfway, but the girl murmurs, "Rope, maybe."

In the distance, I hear voices. Men's voices, and they're calling first in Duran, then Ariminthian, then the common language.

We saw your fire. We're here to help. Come out, honey, no harm will come to you.

The girl and I trade looks.

"Right." I glance upward. "I'll climb to that first branch, then

I'll tie knots in this rope and lower it down to you. You'll climb the rope using the knots till you get up there, and then it should be easy to step from branch to branch like a ladder, high enough so the canopy hides us. We pull the rope up behind us, and even if they know we're here, they won't be able to get to us."

The girl is quiet, and over the jungle sounds, we hear a dim crashing. Pirates are coming through the undergrowth not so carefully.

"Will this really work?" she asks.

"I guess you'll have to trust me." I fit my fingers into the grooves in the bark, but when I glance back at her, she looks kind of lost, like a little kid on their first day of nursery. "Hey. I'm Cora. Remember? What's your name?"

The girl doesn't answer right away. She frowns like she really has to think about it. Finally she ventures, "Vivienne?"

"Right, Vivienne, I'm going up. Then you are coming up. We are going to be safe in the tree, the pirates will sail away without finding us, and then you can go back to your corner of this island and I will go back to mine. Fair?"

She nods again. It's a little eerie, the way she doesn't talk. But there's no time to care, and I shinny up the tree quick as a whistle.

Every kid has to take invasion readiness training, and most of us complain about it. It's hard and scary and cold, and we just want to start our war work. Not everyone is like Kess, who wouldn't shut up about how great it is to pee outside.

But now I'm thanking Sergeant Bale every time my fingers

find a handhold. Every time my legs push me up. He refused to take *I can't* for an answer, no matter how many times he had to show us something, how late he had to stay.

Before long, I'm sitting on the branch. Below, Vivienne paces around the base of the tree, her neck craned up at me.

For the longest moment, I consider leaving her there. Just climbing higher and ignoring her inevitable yelling, but not so high that I'd miss watching the pirates find her.

According to the official reports, my oldest brother died instantly from a single bullet to the head. This was what was written in the letter we received from the Department for the Defense of Liberty—the war department, but we're not supposed to call it that—and what the smartly dressed lieutenant said when he turned up on our doorstep with that folded flag. *Never suffered. Died a hero.*

But a few weeks later, an envelope was pushed through our mail slot. No stamp, no return address, no fingerprints. Inside was an unredacted copy of the after-action report of what really happened on that beach, signed by an Ariminthian commander.

That was bad enough, but the back was stamped *Embrace Peace*. Those activist toolbags are always doing stuff like this, trying to turn people against the war by *raising awareness*, as if losing your brother is going to do anything but make you more committed to winning. Everyone calls them Embrace Piss for a reason.

My mom was the one who opened the envelope. She fainted

from the shock and hit her head on the desk on her way to the floor, and she was in and out of bed and the hospital for the better part of a year.

One more reason to never want to embrace anything but complete and total victory, come what may.

Vivienne clearly didn't have any invasion readiness training, or she'd know that she could give my location away to the pirates, but they'd have to *really* care to figure out a way to get me out of this tree, and considering the canopy, there's a very good chance I could escape from tree to tree until they tired of the chase.

Besides, they might not care at all. Not when they already had a captive.

I grip the rope holding the valise to my shoulders. It's not every day I'm able to strike back against the enemy.

Vivienne peers up at me, then glances toward the racket in the jungle that's getting louder by the moment.

She has it coming. She's Ariminthian. She wouldn't hesitate to do the same to me.

At this point, there's no shame in anything you do.

I hope that's true, because I'm about to help the enemy.

I am swearing in a low mutter as I slither out of the rope holding the valise on my back, wedge the black case securely into a Y in the tree just above my head, and cinch one end of the rope around the thickest part of the branch. Once that's done, I find the other end and start tying knots every foot or so.

It's easy at first, but grows considerably harder as I get to the middle of the rope and have to wrestle it and fight my own knots—all while the crashing in the jungle grows closer.

Still swearing, I tie the last knot and fling the whole rope down so it dances in front of her. She grabs high—first smart thing I've seen her do—then settles one foot and then the other on the bottom knot. The rope sways perilously, and she stifles a squeal as it swivels and takes her with it.

The pirates will find us at any moment. They'll see her swinging there, and they'll have the rope to climb, so they'll get me, too.

Use what the land gives you.

The land is giving me jack-all right now, but the sea gave me this black valise with the lock I can't pry.

I tug it out of its spot. Vivienne has been eyeing this case, so it must contain something valuable.

Right now it's going to save us both.

I grab it by the handle and heave it up and out, as hard as I can. It sails a good distance before landing with a brushy *thump*.

There's a moment of odd stillness. Vivienne clings to the rope, eyes wide. The pirates stop their crashing, and I hold my breath. Only the jungle responds, and it's with a flutter of wings and a battering of *whirrrrrrrr-cheeeecheeeecheeeee* that's agitated and worried and scared.

Then the crashing moves away from us.

Vivienne has stopped climbing. She's staring after the pirates. Toward where I flung the valise.

I make an impatient gesture, and she blinks hard like she's trying not to cry. Then, slowly, she starts climbing again, until she's finally close enough to haul herself gracelessly over the branch, floppy like a stuffed toy. She's panting hard and sickly pale. I haul up the rope hand over hand, and when I have it all, I untie it from the branch and wind it across my body for easier climbing.

We'll likely need it to get down, but I don't think I want to let Vivienne choose when she does that.

"Up we go." I point to the series of branches that ladder into the canopy and out of sight of the ground.

"But they'll find—"

Vivienne bites it back, and in that moment I *know* there's something worth having in that case. Something that's locked away for a reason.

"—us," she finishes halfheartedly, and then turns her eyes upward, toward the climb we still must make.

"Not if we move now," I reply, and I go first. If she falls out of this tree, I'll be damned if she takes me with her.

VIVIENNE

THE PIRATES ARE arguing.

I don't dare look down, but I can tell that they are five, and far enough distant that their voices are garbled through the thick damp heat of the jungle.

Three of the pirates are Ariminthian. *Three.*

It doesn't make sense. Pirates are Duran. Everyone knows that. It's the language they beg in as the sea takes them.

I'm clutching the trunk of the tree we climbed, pressing my whole self against it, every breath coming in a whistle and going out a prayer.

It's good, I keep telling myself. If the Duran girl threw the case away, she clearly doesn't know what's inside.

I can't quite hear what the pirates are fighting over. Something about the signal fire. Whether it's worth it to search the island.

I don't think they found the penner. If they had, one of them would have said something. He'd have smashed it open and found the seal. It would be easy to mistake the gilt for real gold, especially when the royal jeweler inset so many precious stones. It would be easy for a pirate to pocket it and melt it down without ever knowing what he had.

That means the seal in its case is still down there, somewhere in the undergrowth, and I mean to find it. Even if I have to search every day this island grants me.

At length, the voices fade to footsteps, and the footsteps into jungle sounds. I want to slump, but I don't dare. One wrong move and I'll fall to my death.

Beside me, the Duran girl is trembling like the princess when she's been too long at a dinner party.

"We should be all right if we stay here," the girl whispers. "I am *not* moving from this tree till they're long gone."

I wonder if she means to sleep here. I certainly don't, and I also don't want to sit for days with the enemy. Already the quiet is becoming uncomfortable. Her with her dirty fingernails and stolen trousers, and me doing all I can not to look down.

"Besides, I haven't seen much of anything worth plundering on the beaches. They'll figure that out soon and leave." She laughs lightly. "Unless you've got a bunch of treasure stashed away or something."

I go still and cold. Not for myself. For the princess.

If the Duran girl could find my camp by following my

footprints in the sand, the pirates can as well. I never did muddle them. The island is supposed to take care of things like that.

The trunks and sea rations are of little consequence—the island can provide more—but they will find her shrine.

They may walk past it. Or they may kick it to bits for the sport of it.

The Ariminthians among them will know what it is they're looking at, that there ought to be valuables buried deep within. True Ariminthians would never desecrate a shrine, but these men have been corrupted by Durans and their greed. They are pirates now. They are capable of anything.

If they move so much as a petal, my mistress will no longer have a home here. She will never, *never* let me rest easy. Not here. Not anywhere.

My mistress never wanted to come on the *Burying Ground*. I'm the one who convinced her. One day I was carrying a load of laundry down to the pump yard when the king's consort nodded me into an alcove.

The Durans are insisting that the signing take place on a ship at sea, he told me. *If the whole royal family is not present, their lot won't even get on board.*

Right away I saw the problem. The princess would dig in her heels. She would hide beneath her bedclothes and be ill, just like I suggested that first day we met. She might even *make* herself ill with worry.

We are all working on her, the consort went on. *Myself. The*

*king. Even the Royal Mother is coming in from her villa. We know
Aubrey would rather stay home, but she can't this time. If she does, the
Durans will cry foul and abandon the peace table. The war will go on.*

The war will get worse. He doesn't say as much, but that's
what he means.

I have always liked the king's consort. He's the kindest
person in the royal household, and even though he must know
I belong in the darkest corners of the scullery with the rest of
the debtors, he has never treated me poorly. He goes out of his
way to make eye contact, to thank me when I clear a dish or
fetch some small object. He understands my mistress as well,
in a way her other father does not. He doesn't huff and sigh
when she's *too ill* to go to dinner parties, and he intervenes
gracefully and tactfully if she's floundering in a conversation.

So when he asked me to convince my mistress that there
was no danger, that the *Burying Ground* would be as safe as a
summer picnic, I agreed.

I was the one she saw every day. That was by design on
her part, but also because her fathers were busy with matters of
state and her sisters loved to do things that made her anxious
or uncomfortable.

I told my mistress that the trip would last just a few weeks.
She wouldn't have to talk to anyone. Just stand there with her
family in a respectable gown and perhaps a pretty hat. The
Durans simply needed her to be present. To be seen. Then
there'd be peace.

Imagine that. There'd be peace.

No more bombings or explosions or sabotage. No more endless barrages from war machines. No more acrid smoke rising in ominous pillars from different quarters of the city. No more body counts.

Peace, the princess whispered.

Both of us sat for a moment, thinking how that would be.

Then Princess Aubrielle Melisande Felicity Tiralie Vivienne of Ariminthia lifted her chin, squared her shoulders, and whispered that she'd do it. She'd get on that ship.

She'd help win peace.

I press my forehead against the tree trunk. This is not the peace she hoped to win, but it's a peace I hope she is enjoying.

It's a peace I'm going to protect.

I peel my arms away from the tree and shift my weight along the branch. I still can't bring myself to look down, but I failed to save the princess before. I will save her now or die trying.

"Hey, what are you doing?" The Duran girl reaches a hand toward me, but I bat it away.

"I am climbing down," I tell her. "Leave me be."

"Good luck with that." She holds both hands up in an overdramatic flourish. Then she peers at me and asks, "But why?"

I ignore her and cling to the branch as I gingerly edge my legs over.

"Wait. Does this have something to do with that suitcase I threw?"

I go still, then curse myself for it. She crows in delight, then starts shinnying down the tree while I'm still folded over the branch.

She will find the royal penner while I'm trapped here, and that cannot happen. I must send her away so I have time to secure it, and there's but one thing that might sway her.

"It's—it's the food." I silently beg the island's pardon. "I have meat and bread. The pirates will take it all. I want to hide it from them, and I will give you some if you help me."

The Duran girl frowns. "This sounds like a trick."

"No trick. There is plenty." I grit my teeth and hiss, *"Please."*

She is thinking. I can see every last argument she is making with herself pass over her face. At last she sighs harshly and says, "*Half.* You will give me half of everything you have. Got it?"

"Yes. Yes. I will give you half, but we must hurry."

The girl glides her fingers and toes into the bark. "If you don't come help me, I'm taking everything."

"I will help, but I cannot climb as fast as you. I will come as soon as I can."

"Make sure all your handholds and toeholds are good before you let go to take a new one." She grins at me, sudden and unexpected. "Otherwise you'll beat me to the ground."

I bristle, but I don't think it's a threat. It's a . . . joke?

I pretend I don't hear her and start making my way down. Below, I can hear the faint crunch and shuffle of limbs and leaves, and when I dare a glance, she's already on the ground, peering up at me. The climbing rope she promised is secured to the bottom-most branch. Hopefully, we can come back for it. It's hard to believe the pirates will see any value in old ratline.

My heart is hammering, and my fingers and toes are burning numb. I reach for a handhold and shift my weight slowly, slowly.

"Hey? Vivienne? You're taking forever. Why don't I run ahead to your camp? I can start hiding stuff and you can catch up."

My fingers slip, and I squeal and scrabble and catch myself with my knee, sharp, painful. When I can breathe again, when my heart is back in my chest, the clearing is empty.

Durans might be greedy, but at least they are predictable.

Already this girl is asking too many questions about the royal penner. That means she has every intention of finding it once the pirates are gone. She even said as much. *Don't think you can just keep whatever I give you.*

As if the royal seal was ever hers to give or keep. It belongs to the island, and therefore the princess. The sea sent it here so I could save Ariminthia by bringing it to her mother.

But first I need to find it.

CORA

I MOVE THROUGH the jungle, keen and single-minded. Meat and bread. Meat and bread. Even my footsteps echo that promise in my ears.

If this is a trick, I swear I will bring the war to Vivienne in a way she will not like.

Going over the beach would be easier, but that's where the pirates will be, scouting for washed-up loot. Instead I keep the water in flickers through the brush on my left but stay just inside the tree line, ready to duck for cover if need be.

I stay calm. I take my bearings. Honestly, invasion readiness training might be the best ten weeks I ever spent. Even if Kess was the one who got the best time in the wilderness drop and went around bragging to anyone who'd listen and wearing her ribbon every day and generally being insufferable about it in the weeks before she moved away and gave us all some peace and freaking quiet.

It feels like forever before I spot the uprights of some kind of structure. It was clearly made by a person who isn't me, and when I peer through the undergrowth, I can make out an arbor of some kind. I remember it from that day I went to Vivienne's camp, but then I was too busy looking for people to pay it much mind. Under it there's a scattering of rocks heaped over with big jungle flowers, with a gray blanket folded neatly at one end. The rocks are all the same size, shiny and blindingly white, arrayed in a precise spiral that makes me think of seashells.

There's not much of anything else—except the trunks.

They're big and painted black, and there must be fully a dozen, tipped on their sides with the contents arrayed across the sand as if everything is spilling out naturally.

There's some clothing and blankets and a scattering of things like soap and teacups, but most of the stuff looks like wood shavings and bricks. At first I'm not sure what to make of it, but when I get closer, I realize it's food.

Vivienne was not lying about the food.

No wonder she looks so tidy and well-fed. She's got dried meat and fruit leather and some kind of crumbly biscuit that tastes like sweetened sawdust but is hitting my clamoring belly like a toasty fire after a rainstorm.

Eating takes all my focus. Grab some dried meat. Chew on it while reaching for some peanuts. Crack open the shells and crunch down the nuts while tearing open another parcel of dried fish.

The world is narrow. I have a task, and it's to fill my stomach.

When the edge is off, I snap back. Pirates. I'm here to keep this food from them. Half of it is mine now.

I cram one more strip of dried meat into my mouth, then grab a sea bag and start filling it. It's a moment before I realize it's Alivarda's sea bag, which Vivienne stole from my camp, but whatever. What's important now is the food. There's a lot of it, and soon the bag is bulging. I lay a piece of sailcloth flat and start piling goods in the middle with the idea of making a bundle, but there's simply too much here.

There's no way I can hide all this stuff before the pirates find it. They're going to help themselves to every last dried apple and biscuit, and there's no way to know how long before an actual rescue ship will get here. How long the pirates will stay, when I can get another signal fire going.

Whether that's even a good idea.

"All this stuff," I say aloud, because once the pirates sail away, Vivienne and I will be alone on this island again, and I don't see how I can go back to daleberries and water once my share runs out. Not when an Ariminthian has somehow gotten all this stuff and can possibly get more.

I don't see how I'm going to move through my days knowing there's an Ariminthian here, and we are still at war.

The sailcloth bundle is almost too heavy to lift, so I fling out a bedsheet and start piling it with biscuits, dried fruit, bags of nuts. It's not even halfway full when Vivienne pushes her way out of the brush. Her eyes go from me to the overstuffed sea bag to the goods still lying in the sand.

She might have promised me half her food when we were in the tree, when she wanted something from me, but she might be changing her mind now. It's not like Ariminthians are known for following the rules.

"This is going to take forever." I gesture helplessly to the trunks and the stuff still displayed across the sand like this is a freaking general store. "Why didn't you just leave everything put away?"

Without a word, Vivienne picks up a palm-size silver bowl and pushes past me toward the beach. She hurries all the way down to the waterline, then backs up, reshaping the sand with the bowl's curved end to press away our tracks.

"What are you even *doing*?" I call after her. "It's too late for that now! The pirates are going to search—ughhh! Never mind."

I grab the sailcloth bundle and try to heft it, but my knot comes loose and food start spilling out. Swearing, I tug the whole sheet of canvas like a sledge back toward the jungle, step by tedious step.

Vivienne is watching, still holding the bowl. She makes no move to help.

Always listen to your gut, Sergeant Bale said. *If something feels off, it probably is.*

I stop. I let the sailcloth go.

Vivienne knew there'd be too much stuff to hide easily and quickly. If the first thing she did was muddle our footprints, she must believe she can hide her camp from the pirates. If that's all it was going to take to keep the food safe, why promise me half if I'd agree to help do something unnecessary? Something that was going to be impossible anyway?

"Yeah, I don't like this." I keep my eyes on Vivienne as I stoop to pick up Alivarda's bulging sea bag. "I'll come back for my half later. If it's even still here. But I'm at least taking something now."

"No." All at once she goes feral. "I don't care about the food, but the bag does not belong to you. It stays here."

"You're the one who stole it from—"

Over the shushing of the water and the distant cry of the seabirds comes the crunch of footsteps in the jungle.

Coming closer.

Did I—did I leave a *trail* for the pirates to follow?

Vivienne turns to me, and the look on her face is nothing short of panicked.

"Right. Okay." I'm rattled, thinking as fast as I can. Picturing Sergeant Bale shaking his head in utter disappointment, Kess behind him gloating. "The pirates might keep going if they don't think there's any camp here. I almost didn't see it myself. What I spotted was . . ."

The arbor. The arbor and the canopy of boughs and then those rocks and flowers.

Which means all of it has got to go.

I'm reaching for the first upright when someone shoves me from behind and I go sprawling. I hit the sand hard and scramble, but it's not a pirate standing over me.

It's Vivienne. She looks absolutely murderous.

"Don't you touch her," she growls.

"Her—what are you talking about?" I fling a gesture at the arbor. "The pirates will see it and find this camp. This food!"

"I don't care. Back up." Vivienne puts herself between me and the arbor. She's ready to fight.

Oh.

Oh.

If it's a fight she wants, she will have it.

VIVIENNE

WITHOUT FANFARE, THE Duran girl shoves me to one side. She pulls down the uprights of the arbor and flings them, then lashes her foot through the flowers and stones.

I am on her.

I think I'm screaming.

Let the pirates find me. They will find the Duran girl, too, and they will have no mercy. Nothing they do to me matters now.

The Duran girl is strong and she knows how to fight. Neither is true of me. I am face-first in the sand and she is sitting on me. One hand on the back of my head, pressing my cheek against the grit. I can't reach my arms back to hit her. I can't shift my body enough to get free.

I am still screaming.

"Shut up!" the girl hisses in my ear, cramming my face down harder. "What is *wrong* with you?"

Everything. Everything is wrong.

I barely feel the royal seal gouging into my chest. Finding it seemed so important just minutes ago, when I was pawing through the damp undergrowth for the case and then using royal birthdays as lock tumbler patterns till one—the king's consort's—caused it to glide open. Spending precious moments to tear the purple lining from the case to make a string to carry the seal safely around my neck, beneath my clothes, against my heart.

But it doesn't matter now that my mistress has been severed from the only place she's ever known peace. When she and the island will both turn on me.

The weight lifts off my back, but I press my forehead to the sand and weep. I weep like I haven't since I found myself here, alive when I shouldn't be. Alone when I couldn't bear to be.

I tried so hard. All I wanted was to do right by her.

"Hey." Something shakes my shoulder. The Duran girl, her eyes big and earnest like she hasn't just murdered the princess all over again. "Let's go."

All I wanted was to finally know peace.

"Get up," the girl says, simple and firm like she's in any position to give me an order and expect me to follow it. "We have half a chance now if we hurry."

Sand sticks to my wet cheeks. From the corner of my eye, I can see a trampled piece of ground with sad, wilted flowers scattered like limp corpses.

"Hey, what is—oh!" A pirate pushes his way out of the jungle. He's shirtless, huge, and hulking, and when he sees us, he crashes to a stop and hollers over his shoulder, "Here's a few!"

More pirates pour from the jungle behind him. The big pirate sheathes his cutlass and holds a hand toward us, a gentling hand, steadying, like you might toward a dish about to fall from a table.

The Duran girl lets the sea bag she's holding slide from her shoulder. "Run."

Not ten heartbeats since her shrine is destroyed, and pirates find me. This is the beginning of the end.

Somehow I'm on my feet and stumbling back. Then back again. Alongside a *Duran* of all people.

"Don't be afraid, honey," says the first pirate.

"We're here to help you," adds another, bigger and sunburned, covered in scars and missing an ear.

My heart is racing and I press a hand against it. Against the royal seal of Ariminthia and the aching place on my body where it dug in.

Where it left a mark.

"Run," Cora hisses. Somehow she is still here. She has not left me to them. So this time I do it. I turn on my heel and heave myself forward.

A wide scarred hand comes at me, grabbing, but my fists are still full of sand from clawing for a handhold when Cora held me down. I fling those handfuls at pirate faces, and they stagger long enough for us to dart through them. Past them.

And we run.

I leave everything behind. Food, water, trunks, supplies—and her. Princess Aubrielle Melisande Felicity Tiralie Vivienne of Ariminthia, who will never again know rest.

BLADE, BOWL, TWINE

CORA

I DON'T THINK. I just run. I don't care if Vivienne is behind me. I have a task and I focus on it.

Get clear.

Something behind me is breathing heavily. I put my head down and go. My feet hit the sand with tiny *pish-pish*es.

A stitch shoots up my side, and when I press a hand against it, I catch a glimpse of flying purple fabric. Vivienne. I risk a glance but I don't see any pirates chasing us.

After rounding the third headland, I stagger to a stop near the tree line and fight to catch my breath. Vivienne falls still at my side and gasps for air. My lungs are burning and my legs ache, but the beach stretches empty behind us.

"I think we lost them," I finally manage.

Vivienne laughs a little, harsh and cruel. She's watching me sidelong in a way that makes me move a step away from her. Her eyes are red, and there's something coiled and dangerous about her, like machinery cranked three turns too many.

"For now. Soon enough they'll hunt us down. It's likely been a while since the crew has had any . . . fun." She laughs again, but it's a chilling sound.

I know how they'll catch us, too. How I'd do it. All the pirates have to do is station a guard over every freshwater spring on the island. There can't be too many. We'll be dead in days without drinking water.

"Maybe if you hadn't attacked me for no reason, we'd have some supplies right now," I growl.

"Doesn't matter," she whispers, but I don't think she's talking to me. She looks like she's about to fly into pieces, and I take another step away because she's right. Even with a sea bag full of dried meat and biscuits, without water we're done for.

Your first priority is survival.

Wait. I've done this before. This is the wilderness drop.

First, assess your surroundings. You are determining whether the place you're in right now is safe or whether you need to move immediately.

I've never been to this part of the island, but it's not that different from my home camp. There's a stretch of sand, empty but for driftwood and shells, and a dense wall of jungle that hopefully contains some daleberry bushes and a freshwater spring.

Right now I'm safe, but we left a trail over the sand that even a little kid could follow. I wish I could blame Vivienne, but that one's all me. Just like the trail I somehow left through the jungle for the pirates.

Once you are out of immediate danger, identify what you have to work with and where your pain points will be.

I must have dropped the sea bag at some point—stupid— but Alivarda's clothes are still on my back and his knife is in my pocket.

Then there is Vivienne, still trembling, still breathing hard, who refused to listen when I was trying to help her by hiding her camp and her food from the pirates.

I turn on my heel and head for the jungle, but I haven't gone ten steps when she's at my elbow, then in my path.

"You built the fire to signal a ship, yes?" Her voice is steadier now, but her posture is still violent. "And you plan to try again? Once the pirates sail away?"

I nod, slow and wary.

"I've changed my mind. I want to leave, too. I will help you." Vivienne stares hard at the sand and growls, "Even though we are at war."

There are no rules for the wilderness drop. It's meant to simulate an invasion situation as closely as possible. You may find yourself making choices you might not otherwise make. This is good. This means you are developing the skills you need if you are ever in such a situation.

"Right now there's a cease-fire," I say. "Technically we're not at war."

She frowns like she's thinking it over. Then she nods. "A cease-fire, then."

"Our first priority is survival," I tell her, "and I've been trained, so here's how this is going to work."

Vivienne blinks. "You've been *trained*?"

"Extensively. So listen. You're going to do what I say. You're not going to argue, or you will be on your own. Is that clear?"

Her mouth is hanging open. Not even trying to say words, not in any language. At length she manages to nod once, like her neck is numb.

"All right." I kick at the sand. I was expecting more resistance, and now I have to say something that makes it sound like *extensively* is more impressive than ten weeks of knot tying and orienteering. "We need to get off this beach and find a tactical place to rest. We need to find water, and we need to decide what to do next."

She's still frozen. Still gaping like a fish. Probably she can't believe that a girl has been taught something more complicated than how to fold towels and bake cookies.

I sigh and head into the jungle, and she must snap out of it because I hear her follow, rustling every branch and breaking every twig.

We are going to have to work on that.

When we come to a spring, both of us drink deeply. We sit

on either end of a rotting log while the jungle *whirrrrr*s and *cheeecheeee*s around us.

Vivienne has finally closed her mouth. She is no less tightly wound, but now there's a wariness to her, the skittish kind you'd expect from a stray cat. Nothing of the haughtiness and snobbery I'd expect from an Ariminthian, even a servant who braids hair.

Your secondary priority is sabotage.

There's no way she's had my training, but it would explain a lot. Her unwillingness to let me move her rock pile. Her dragging her feet when the pirates surprised us. Her abrupt about-face in wanting to leave the island. And possibly her agreeing to let me, a Duran, be in charge of our survival.

"Why?" I ask abruptly. "Why did you change your mind about wanting to leave?"

Vivienne squints at nothing. She scrubs a wrist over her eyes. Then she says, "I did not see a purpose for myself. Then I did."

The common language can be weird sometimes. Words don't always translate out of Duran well, and the same is probably true for Ariminthian. It was never meant to be anything more than a trading language, though. Not one pressed into service to aid in diplomacy or negotiation with a hostile power.

Her words sound like something a saboteur might say. Or maybe a servant who just learned she gets to be something other than a servant now that her princess isn't around.

"What will we do next?" Vivienne asks. "You said we would find water, and then we would decide."

"Then *I* will decide." I cut a glance her way, but she doesn't seem angry, so I go on. "Smoke brought the pirates last time. More smoke is our best chance to call one of your people's ships to rescue us."

She looks thoughtful. "The pirates will likely flee as soon as a warship turns up, that's true."

"So we need to evade the pirates and set fires," I say, and as I talk through it I feel more and more relieved. Tasks to focus on. A way forward.

"It could be a while," Vivienne warns.

"A few days?"

"Weeks."

But the way she says it makes me think there's something she isn't telling me, and it has nothing to do with sabotage. Likely it has to do with the very real possibility that those weeks may turn into months.

I know I can last a few days out here, even away from a stable camp and a source of food and water. After Kess, I had one of the best times in the wilderness drop.

But weeks? With nothing but a jackknife and the clothes on my back? Surrounded by pirates starved for fun?

Yes. *Hell* yes, I can do this. And it's going to be on the front page of every newspaper across the republic of Dura, and I am never, *never* going to get tired of telling this story.

Something goes *kerplunkety* at my feet. It's a pile of branches, damp to the touch and covered with moss. Vivienne stands over me, brushing crumbs of bark off her sleeves.

"If we're doing this, let's get started." Her voice is flinty and her eyes far away.

"Agreed. But not here. We don't want to make it easy for them to find this spring."

VIVIENNE

THERE ARE TWO things that keep me from killing her outright.

The first is that I need her. The sea has already sent pirates. Soon my mistress will turn the full wrath of this place on me. There is but one reason left for me to survive, and it hangs around my neck, its edges digging into my breastbone beneath my dress.

The second is that I *cannot* kill her. This is the sea's doing, too. That the only other survivor here is a Duran girl who is stronger than me and faster, and she has been *trained* in these things.

Which means that the minister for counterterrorism was right all along. All those Duran boys and girls caught in the dockyards or near the admiralty with explosives and wire, or mallets, or devices we couldn't begin to guess at. None of them revealed anything useful, not even under torture, but the minister for counterterrorism swore it pointed to one thing.

They are not soldiers, the minister told the king, *but they have been trained by military personnel.*

We didn't catch them all. Every few weeks, there would be a distant explosion and the ground would shake and the air would reek of sulfur, and the princess would sink to her knees and crawl under a table and curl up on herself and panic and babble and sob.

They are young, the minister told the king. *No older than your own children.*

The king put his head in his hands. His face was stone as he ordered each one shot.

I knew the Durans were capable of a lot, but a military training program for children—that seemed like too much.

But here is proof that it's not. She walks in front of me in a murdered cabin boy's stolen clothing, and I am following her because she is the means to an end.

The first fire we set is on a windswept length of beach on the leeward side of the island. I drop the wood in a heap, but Cora kneels and arranges it into a grid with the smallest bits on the bottom and a fat wad of dry grass in the center. Then she grinds the murdered cabin boy's stolen splicing knife down a shiny black rock until sparks leap out.

"C'mon," she grouses from her hands and knees. "Get down here and blow with me."

It won't matter. The island won't help me, and it won't help her, either.

But still I join her. Tiny sparks glow like stars in the nest of moss, then send up the thinnest wisps of smoke. She is patient, blowing careful and steady while making a windbreak with her body. Little wicks of flame emerge, crawling up the small sticks, and soon the fire has well and truly caught. The smoke grows thicker as the fire climbs to larger pieces of wood, and Cora gently stacks more until the structure resembles a tower.

We both watch as the smoke grows heavy and black, pushing straight up in a sturdy, defiant column.

I move to leave, but Cora wanders the beach until she finds a conch shell about the size of her hand. She uses a stick to push coals into the shell. Soon the shell is full, and she nods me toward the jungle, but I'm rooted to the spot.

That shell is the perfect size and shape for holding coals for the next fire. The island gave it to her, just like that.

The island should not be helping her. The *princess* should not be helping her.

Cora tells me to hurry up and heads into the jungle. She holds the shell in front of her like it's made of glass.

I take a moment to erase our footsteps from the sand with the silver bowl that somehow stayed in my pocket when I fled the pirates. I must take care of things like this now, since the island has no plans to.

As I follow Cora, I rustle every branch and pet every leaf, thanking the island for letting me continue to live for one more step, then another. I silently ask it to intercede with the princess, to explain what must look like treason and blasphemy.

I know what I have coming, I beg her, *but please wait till Ariminthia is safe.*

"Hey, could you at least *try* to be quiet?" Cora says over her shoulder. "The pirates have probably found our fire by now, and once they put it out, they're going to figure we went into the jungle. If we're crashing around, they'll find us before we can set more fires."

My heart sinks. The pirates will put out the fire. This one, and the next one, and the next.

For someone trained as a spy and a saboteur, her plan isn't that good.

"And could you *at least* have the courtesy to respond when someone talks to you?"

I am remembering that first day in the palace, how the chatelaine closed the door in my mother's tear-streaked face, dragged me down a rough stone hallway, then shoved me into a dark cabinet that smelled of musty linen. While I wailed and hammered on the hatch with both fists, she told me that when I'd accepted my lot, when I agreed it was just, I could shut my mouth and knock three times. That's how she'd know I was ready to follow the rules.

"Ah." My throat is scratchy. "It's not my custom to speak unless there's something that must be said."

Cora snorts. "Your *custom.* You're not allowed, are you?"

I am remembering how quickly I broke. How quickly I swallowed my tears and scrubbed my eyes and knocked three times on the hatch. *Remunerative servitude* was almost as terrifying as *lèse majesté*, and the chatelaine was not shy about saying them in the same breath with an accusing edge, like I was the one who had betrayed the Crown and not my father.

I am remembering how I repeated the rules after her. How I would conduct myself in the presence of my betters. How I would be silent unless spoken to. How I would anticipate their wants and needs as if they were my own.

How I would never, *never* be allowed to leave the palace. Not for a day. Not for an hour. Not for any reason whatsoever.

Cora has trailed to a stop. She's regarding me now, but not in a cruel way. "Sorry. That was mean. It must be a silver lining for you. Being shipwrecked on this island. You don't have to be anyone's servant. You can just be a regular kid."

My eyes are stinging. There is no way to make her understand. Before the princess, I crouched on a low teetering stool every day in a dim corner of the storehouse, dragging a dull paring knife over turnip after turnip. My bare feet cold against the flagstone, my hands cracking from the juice. No one speaking to me for days at a time, not even the grimy farmer who brought the turnips and carried away the peels for his pigs.

That was to be my life.

I did not *have* to be anyone's servant. It *saved* me.

"Is that why you didn't want to be rescued?" Cora asks. "At first, I mean. I can see why you'd never want to go back to Ariminthia. Hey, maybe you could defect! Depending on what's going on with the cease-fire, I bet Parliament will let you stay in Dura if you tell them secrets from the palace." She shrugs. "I mean, it's not your fault you were born in a crappy place and can't do anything about it."

"Crappy?" The word comes sharp, and I'm about to beg her pardon when I remember that she is Duran and also a murderer twice and thrice and dozens of times over. "Are you . . . are you speaking of Ariminthia?"

"Well. Yeah." Cora sets off through the jungle again. "Monarchy is a stupid system, you know? You have to do what some guy says just because he was born in a palace."

It's pure blasphemy, and I flinch even though I know she is Duran and sees no problem with being governed by any flim-flam man who manages to convince enough empty-headed fools that he should be allowed to govern, regardless of his skills and abilities.

To say nothing of his integrity.

"I mean, what if the guy born in the palace is a giant doofus? What then? What can regular people do to stop him from doing stupid things that aren't good for anyone but himself?"

I could ask the same of her. Durans make such a production about how they vote for their leaders, but that only proves how much they love the war. If they truly wanted the war to end, they'd vote for measures to rein in the industrialists whose greed and self-interest drive them to brutal extraction that leaves nothing but ruin in its wake.

They'd vote for leaders who sought peace.

Yet here we are, this girl and I. This girl who has been

trained for combat, who the island is inexplicably helping. Who the sea not only let live, but brought to this island along with me.

The sea has a plan for each of us and its ways are not for us to know, but for some reason it is testing my resolve, and I am not sure I'm strong enough to see this through.

CHESS TEAM IS not handling boredom well.

We haven't received new orders in almost two weeks, which means we're trapped doing our last assignment, which was to gather intel on pirates. Only there is no new information because apparently the pirates have stopped doing frigging *anything*. They just sail around in neutral waters without rhyme or reason, as if they're pleasure cruising.

My reports are downright sullen, but there are only so many ways you can write *No change in fleet movements. No creditable evidence relating to the* Burying Ground.

It's not like Command to go suddenly quiet, especially for more than a week at a stretch. Usually there's *something* in the dead drop, even if it's a simple order to continue as directed.

"Maybe the opposition whip finally had a psychotic break," Rook says over supper, which is sandwiches and warm water that tastes like the metal pail we keep it in. "Maybe he dissolved Parliament and we have a monarchy now."

King doesn't answer because he has no sense of humor.

I don't answer because it's a little too on the nose. Some of the chatter we've been hearing is downright alarming. It's getting harder to keep pretending that the *Burying Ground* is coming back, but if that's not the case, it becomes a matter of what happened to it.

Ariminthian ships are notoriously hard to sink. It's that special wood they're built with, along with a series of treatments and techniques that covert ops has lost some very good teams trying to learn. The war would have been over *years* ago if we'd found a way to compromise springwood.

"Maybe the opposition whip was murdered by hardliners and they're running things now." I aim my sandwich at Rook. "No way to know till we get our next assignment. If Command asks us to do something really out there, we'll have a clue."

"*You're* a hardliner," Rook replies deadpan, and I give him the finger but also smile so he knows I'm not mad.

He's wrong, though. I'm not one of those fanatics who can't stand the idea that voting sometimes doesn't go their way. The only reason I don't love this treaty is that I'm not sure what the hell I'd do with myself in peacetime. If it's anything like sitting on my hands during a cease-fire, I'll be in bad shape.

I doubt covert ops will ever go away entirely, but peacetime will make what chess team does now a thing of the past. Give me a box of nails, some gelignite, and an old tin jug, and I can ruin a market day with the best of them. There's just no place for someone like me schmoozing for intel in an evening gown at a dinner party.

After supper, I take the encryption device out of its hiding place and spool in a sheet of dissolving paper. Dead center I type just two words:

NOW WHAT?

Not only is it a flagrant breach of protocol, it's also a colossal waste of paper.

One of three things will happen. Nothing, which leaves chess team pretty much where we are now. We could get new orders. Or I'll get a summons demanding that I turn up in person to explain myself and who the hell I think I am.

I hope it's a summons, even though it would get me an ass-chewing.

A summons would mean the CO is still running the place, which means things back home haven't gone completely sideways.

New orders? That could go either way, depending on how sideways and who's holding the reins.

VIVIENNE

I AM LOST without her shrine.

I am almost thankful for Cora, for the fires we build every day to draw a gunship and the trip wires we set every evening to keep pirates from surprising us in the night. I am thankful for simple tasks like gathering fruit, loading handfuls into our pockets side by side, wordless.

I remind myself I am not doing for Cora, not like I did for my mistress.

But if I am not doing for Cora, and I am no longer able to do for the princess, then who am I doing for?

After a few days, Cora wants to return to my camp. She says if we're quick—and lucky—we may be able to salvage some of the rations before the pirates take everything. I tell her I'm too frightened to go with her, but that is only partly true, and it's not pirates I fear.

I am not surprised when Cora returns empty-handed.

Already the island and the sea conspire.

A few days after that, Cora decides to teach me to build fires. She says it's so I can make myself useful and not just stand there with a bonehead look on my face, but she is almost excited as she explains how to lay sticks in a grid and how to choose wood that's damp but not too damp. When my first few grids of sticks are too large or too small, or they topple and make a terrifying flaming mess across the sand, she does not mock or berate me. She whoops and laughs with something close to joy, then cheerfully tells me to try again.

"You're getting pretty good at fires," Cora says to me one morning. "Let's split up today and each build separate ones. That'll give us twice as many chances to get a ship's attention. What do you think?"

I am remembering how the princess would share her desserts with me. She would show me her drawings and admire mine, and she made sure I had enough blankets when the weather turned chilly.

But I cannot, not ever, remember her asking what I thought about something.

My father did. He'd catch my eye over the breakfast table, my mother already at work sewing sea bags, and he'd ask what I thought about a swim, a walk by the quayside, a trip to the market.

"Well?" Cora pops a few more berries in her mouth. She's smeared with mud to keep the insects at bay. We both are.

"You can talk, you know. Whenever you want. I actually kind of wish you would. It's creepy."

Creepy doesn't translate well into the common language. I glance at the ground, because a lizard or insect comes to mind with that word, but the look about Cora isn't one of disgust or fear.

Rather, she's the image of the princess at a dinner party where her sisters have been whisked away into conversations or dancing and now she's alone at her place at the table or at the edge of the group, alone in the crowded hall.

If I didn't know better, I'd say Cora looks painfully out of her depth.

"I think it's a good idea," I reply. "I will set fires on my own today."

Cora carefully parcels half the coals into a second shell, one that the island gives her easily, without a fuss. She heads east and I go north.

As I walk, I whisper to my mistress. *I know how to make fires now. I no longer need her. Why is she even still alive?*

I come across a place where the sea has sent plenty of driftwood. There are no footprints here, neither old nor new, so this is not a place the pirates have been.

The sea brought this wood. The island kept it safe and drew me here.

"Just give me a sign," I ask aloud, pleading with the island, with her, with the sea, even though I know none of their ways are for me to know.

I grid the sticks and pile the tinder. I pour the coals and blow gently and steadily. It's not long before my fire is perfect, the smoke thick and black.

If there are Royal Navy vessels anywhere nearby, they will come to investigate.

I shield my eyes with one hand, but the horizon is empty. Nothing but that faint fuzzy place where sea and sky greet each other.

I've learned it's a smart idea to wait to collect coals till the fire burns low, so I mark the tide line and dig with my hands for cockles to pass the time. The wet sand is soothing, the water around my ankles warm like bathwater.

I have several handfuls before I realize that no one told me to collect cockles. I did it on my own.

If this works, if we draw a ship with our fires, if it survives or outwits the pirates and we're able to board, I will return to Ariminthia and hand the seal to the Royal Mother and save my homeland from civil war.

Then I will return to the palace.

Those were the terms, after all, and my mother made her mark to them willingly. My father had already been taken away and he would pay with his life, but lèse majesté does not end with the guilty party, especially not when it comes to standing against the war. My mother could not afford the fine and she could not face hard labor in the galleys, because children left alone vanish quickly into bilges or brothels. There was just one other way for what was left of our family to offer compensation.

You will be safe in royal service, she told me. *They will take care of you always.*

Princess Aubrielle Melisande Felicity Tiralie Vivienne of Ariminthia was not the easiest person to get along with, but she did not care that my father was a traitor to the Crown and I'd been bound into royal service to pay his debts.

Without her to safeguard me, I will disappear into the storehouse corner with the turnips and the cold floor.

The cockles are fat and beautiful. I rinse them, then put them in my pockets. They soak through almost immediately, but we can boil two or three at a time in my little bowl. They will keep us going far better than berries alone.

The fire has burned down sufficiently. No one tells me this. I decide it for myself.

I collect coals in the shell and move on. I have not felt untethered like this since I was a child.

It is unsettling, but not entirely unpleasant.

CORA

THIS IS NOTHING like the wilderness drop.

At the end of that, I was sitting at my kitchen table putting away a good bowl of soup. Sergeant Bale shook hands with my parents and tousled my hair. He said it always made him smile to see girls do so well. The next day I woke up in my own bed, cozy under a pile of quilts, and got ready for my first day of war work at the nursery.

Every day I wake up now, I'm sore and damp from sleeping on the ground on a godforsaken island swarming with pirates. My whole self is ablaze with bug bites, and smearing myself with mud helps only a little. There's no hot soup, just daleberries and cockles we slurp down gritty and half-raw. My only company is an Ariminthian girl with a length of twine in her pocket, and sometimes I catch her looking at me like she'd very much like to choke the life out of me with it.

"The best part about being rescued?" I murmur to the reporters who have gathered in my head, notepads at the ready, leaning forward. "Besides ten hot baths and a giant vat of fried chicken?"

I paw through the jungle, looking for an empty stretch of beach. My hair is crawling.

"Seriously, though, the best part of being rescued has got to be standing in front of you all today, making sure Dura knows what happened. Finishing the work we started on the *Burying Ground*. Making sure some good came out of all that loss." I scrub at a bug bite and squint at the slivers of sky. "Being a symbol, you know?"

The reporters lean forward. They are hanging on my every word.

"Poor Vivienne was useless in the jungle," I tell them. "If it wasn't for Sergeant Bale, I don't think we would have survived."

We. Poor Vivienne.

There's no way around the *we*.

Vivienne was also on the *Burying Ground*. She knows as well as I do that the storm happened before the treaty could be signed.

My dad always said that Ariminthians were unreasonable. They couldn't stand anything not going their way, and they were not afraid to shut down negotiations without fanfare.

Only, Vivienne has been following my instructions to draw a ship's attention and avoid the pirates, too. She's not happy about it, that much is clear, but she's had every chance to walk away and she's not taking any of them.

After each of us sets our morning fires, we meet at a spot we've been calling the point. From here, we can keep tabs on the pirate ship where it lies at anchor. It's been—I don't know, maybe a week—since they arrived and the ship is still riding high in the water.

I know very little about boats, but even I know that means there's not much in the holds.

The beach is littered with tents and cooking fires and pirates doing small, ordinary things. They come and go into the jungle, different groups at staggered times. Searching for us.

"I don't understand," Vivienne murmurs. "There's no loot. No captives to use for fun. There's no reason for them to stay."

All at once I don't want to look at pirates anymore, so I lead the way into the jungle, near one of the freshwater springs that the pirates haven't found yet. We make a small smokeless fire and boil cockles in Vivienne's silver bowl.

With both of us setting fires, it won't be long until a ship arrives to scatter the pirates and rescue us. I need to know what Vivienne plans to tell people about the treaty when she gets home.

I need us to have the same story.

"Hey," I say, and she turns toward me where she's perched on a mossy log. She doesn't look tidy anymore. I probably look worse. "I've been wondering something. How did you end up on the *Burying Ground*?"

"Um. Walked up the gangplank?"

I smile without meaning to. The common language strikes

again. "I mean, the terms of the signing said only the royal family had to come. Not servants."

"I chose to come," she replies. "My place is at the princess's side."

I can't help but notice she said *is*, like the princess is still alive somehow. Kind of like I can't quite let go of the idea that my parents made it to another island, or they've been rescued already and they're hogging my spotlight back in Dura.

It's a small thing to have in common, but it's enough.

"So the princess was . . . your friend," I say.

"You will keep her name *out* of your filthy Duran mouth," Vivienne hisses.

I frown, taken aback. "Yeah. I didn't say her name. I don't even *know* her name."

"Princess Aubrielle Melisande Felicity Tiralie Vivienne of Ariminthia. Who you *murdered*!"

"What?" I'm not sure what's going on here. "She drowned. Like everyone else."

Vivienne turns away and presses her hands to her eyes. She's sobbing, moaning low, and the chill of the shade and the chirring of birds makes me think of my first few nights here, crying hard for my parents, wishing they'd just come get me like I was some little kid in the nursery.

I should say I'm sorry. It's what people say to my parents when they hear about my brothers. It's what you say to anyone who has that candle in their front window that means they just got That Letter from the war department.

I'm not sorry, though. I don't know if I even can be.

"I was ready to be happy here," Vivienne whispers. "Just the princess and me. She would ask the island to send whatever I need. I would make all the offerings. We would have grown together over the years, so close you couldn't tell where I ended and the island began." She pulls in a long shuddering breath. "But you took that all away and now I am alone and she is helping you and *I don't know why.*"

"You . . ." I try to say it as nicely as I can. "You are not making sense right now."

"She is helping you," Vivienne repeats in a thick voice. "Even though you desecrated her shrine."

"Shrine? You mean that thing with the rocks and flowers?"

"Yes." Every word a dagger. "That thing with the rocks and flowers."

I fish the cockles out of the bowl with a twig and lay them on a flat rock to cool while I try to think of what to say. We learned in school that the Ariminthians are superstitious. They believe the sea is alive somehow and can think and decide things, which I guess makes sense for people who spend so much time near water and on boats and ships. Apparently, they're superstitious about the dead as well.

"Well, I sure didn't mean to wreck someone's grave," I say.

Vivienne shudders. "Ugh, no! I wouldn't dream of burying her in the *soil*. It was a *shrine*. A memorial. A place for her to be, and a way for her to be present, even when . . ."

I turn my whole attention to dropping a few more cockles

into the bowl and nudging it back into the coals. It's another small thing we have in common—trying to keep someone you care about nearby, like I've been doing with my parents.

Maybe that's why she changed her mind about being rescued. Whatever weird superstition that makes her believe that the princess is part of the island got ruined when I trashed the shrine.

I should feel better about that. How I wrecked something for an Ariminthian.

But right now I need her to listen to me about the treaty.

"You miss her," I say quietly. "You miss your friend."

Vivienne draws back, shocked. "No. No. She was my mistress. I was her lady-in-waiting."

"Ah." I poke the cockle bowl so she won't see me rolling my eyes. "Well. All right. But you were close to her? She was kind of *like* your friend?"

Vivienne pauses, like she's sorting through words in the common language. "Perhaps *like* a friend."

"So you wouldn't want people to say she died for nothing." I pick at the moss on the log. "I don't want people to say that about my parents."

Vivienne frowns but doesn't reply. I'm not sure if this is part of her conditioning or if she just doesn't like what I said.

"So that's why I think we should tell everyone—whoever picks us up, your new king, my new prime minister, our parents, everyone—that the treaty was already signed when the storm hit." I sneak a glance at her. "Right now there's a cease-fire, and if the treaty was signed, it's peace, but if people *don't* think the treaty was signed, there's a good chance they'll go right back to fighting. If everyone remembers the loss of the *Burying Ground* as a sacrifice for peace, they'll want to honor that."

"But the treaty was not signed."

"It *could* be. If we say it was. Think about it. We'd be *heroes*." I lean forward. "Otherwise there'll be no more cease-fire. We're back at war. And I don't know about you, but I'm tired of the war."

Out of habit I glance around nervously, because you can get in real trouble for bad-mouthing the war.

You can say you wish we'd win the war so you could get fresh meat and ice cream. You can say you miss your brother who got hacked to bits on some Ariminthian beach. But what you *can't* say is you're tired of the war, or tired of rationing or wartime restrictions.

Being tired of fighting is how you lose.

But there's a cease-fire. Maybe it's okay to be tired of fighting now that we didn't lose.

Vivienne is still not saying anything. She's sitting broomstick straight, her hands clenched tight in her lap.

"Look, I can't make you tell people that the treaty was signed," I rush on. "But can you at least think about it? Unless it's true what they say about Ariminthians."

"And what do *they* say about Ariminthians?"

"That the reason the war has gone on for so long is because your nobility won't exist without it and so they shut down every negotiation with unreasonable demands," I reply. "There's basically no reason for them if they're not always thinking about war, or planning for war, or sending their bailiffs around to extract taxes to pay for the war. So they tell all of you ordinary people lies about the war so you'll go along with it. And you believe them because you're not allowed to think for yourselves."

Vivienne scoffs, and in that moment she sounds like Kess whenever I'd insist I could beat her this time.

She sounds like a normal kid.

"But I don't care if it's true or not," I rush on, because maybe that was the wrong thing to say. "If your princess was here, what would she want you to do?"

Vivienne looks away. "My mistress always hated the war."

"Maybe that's why she's helping me, then," I say. "Maybe she even *wanted* me to ruin the shrine. So you'd change your mind about being rescued and go back to Ariminthia and tell everyone the treaty was signed so the war she hated so much could finally end."

Vivienne's face is turning the sort of red that reminds me she has razor-sharp twine in her pocket.

But all she says is *oh*. It's barely a breath.

That's when we hear it—a low rumbling. There's an odd smell in the air, too. If I was home, I'd think it was smoke from one of the metal smithies.

"A storm?" I ask, even though the sky is blue between the branches.

Vivienne shakes her head. "Cannon."

In a trice, we're sprinting through the jungle toward the point. It's one of the few places on the island where there's something of a cliff. It's steep, perhaps twice my height, and rocky. The beach below is rougher, the sand less silky, more broken shells.

Sure enough, the pirate ship is still anchored offshore, but there's another ship, too. Even at a distance I can tell it's flying Ariminthia's red and yellow flag.

The metal smell is stronger here, and as we watch, a handful of gleaming cannon appear through the gunports. There's a low *boom-rumble*, and a twist of smoke drifts up as the cannon leap back through the openings.

The pirates on the island are scrambling. They're piling into the ship's boat that's beached nearby, leaving everything behind, and on the ship itself, more pirates are hauling ropes and moving sails to make their escape.

My face hurts, and it's a moment before I realize I'm grinning. I never thought I'd be glad to see Ariminthians. Today I am. I will be off this island. Hopefully, there'll be a decent meal. Maybe news of my parents.

"We have to swim for it." Vivienne slides out of her dress and kicks off her shoes.

"No way. They came because of the smoke. They know someone's here. Surely they'll come look for us once the pirates flee."

Vivienne is shaking her head the whole time I'm talking.

"By now the captain is reckoning that he's been tricked. That the pirates were the ones who set the fires, to lure a Royal Navy ship close so they could ransack it for powder and shot."

My throat is choking closed. Because that's what I'd do if I were a pirate and needed that stuff.

The ocean stretches out, churned up from the wind and a million shades of rippling blue. The Ariminthian ship looks impossibly tiny, although it can't be more than a few hundred yards out. Sergeant Bale taught us to hold our breath, and I must have flailed enough in the water after the *Burying Ground* to keep myself from drowning, but there's no way I can make it that far.

"We can signal them," I reply. "There's no way they'll leave us here for the pirates."

The shore is deserted now, strewn with stray lengths of rope and rubbish. The ship's boat is halfway back to the pirate vessel, crammed full of men and riding dangerously low in the water.

"The pirates are weighing anchor." Vivienne stands next to a pile of clothes, wearing nothing but a garment that looks like a camisole stitched to a pair of bloomers. She's securing a gold charm tightly to her wrist with a purple cord. "They will try to sail away, and the Royal Navy will chase them and sink them. It's their standing orders when it comes to pirates. They won't return here. This is our chance. I'm taking it. Are you coming?"

It's a lot of words for her. I look down. My eyes filling with tears as I whisper, "I can't."

"You can't swim that far?"

"I can't swim."

Vivienne's face doesn't change. She regards me for more long moments than it feels like we have. Then she says, "I will swim to the ship. I'll tell them you are here, and they will send a boat to pick you up."

It takes a moment to register. Then it hits all at once, like a drench of cold water. "You're leaving me here to die. That's what this is. Because of what I said about—"

"Do you remember the tree?" she cuts in. "You thought about leaving me on the ground for the pirates to find. Admit it. You did."

It stops me. I could lie. But I don't. "I thought about it."

"You said I'd have to trust you." Vivienne binds her hair back in one long braid and ties it with a strip of purple cloth. "Now you're going to have to trust me."

She doesn't say it mean or snarky, but I'm filled with the most overwhelming hatred. As if it's that easy, to trust someone when you're holding absolutely no cards at all.

Vivienne picks her way down the rocky outcrop, then wades into the sea without a backward glance. The waves pelt and buffet her, and it occurs to me that if she drowns, I'm lost.

Setting fires won't work anymore, as the Ariminthians will be reluctant to investigate them once word of this event gets around.

I have to assume that pirates are already picking up anything usable that came from the *Burying Ground*, here and elsewhere, and soon there'll be nothing left to give searchers an idea where it might have been lost. It will be a million-to-one chance that someone will come to this island for years, and possibly forever.

Vivienne's dark head bobs among the waves, moving slow and steady toward the Ariminthian ship. The distance that didn't look far just moments ago now stretches into forever.

I can't watch. Just in case her head slips under and never comes back up. So instead I look down at the rocky stretch of beach below. I count the driftwood logs that the tide can't quite reach, that must have been pushed here during a storm like the one that sank the *Burying Ground*. I count the big boulders that haven't been turned to pebbles by the incessant surf. I count the shovels propped against the cliff wall.

Wait. Shovels?

Behind me something goes *crackle-snap*, and a burly pirate comes out of the brush. He's struggling beneath the weight of a sea chest.

The point is exposed. There's nowhere to go. Nowhere to hide.

"Hurry up!" the pirate calls over his shoulder, low and impatient.

Sergeant Bale said we were never to directly engage the enemy. He kept reminding us that we were not soldiers, that if we were using our training, it meant that we were more valuable than soldiers, and that meant we were more valuable alive.

But one day, we had a different instructor. He called himself Sergeant Black—definitely not his real name—and he dimmed the lights, had us sit on the floor in a circle, and taught us how to defend ourselves if it was ever necessary.

Pressure points.

Vulnerable areas.

The element of surprise.

There is a very good chance that your enemy will underestimate you, Sergeant Black told us. *There is a moment he will hesitate. That is your moment. Use it well.*

The pirate locks eyes with me. He doesn't soothe or sweet-talk me like the last one. Instead his jaw drops, and he grips the chest he's holding like it's full of treasure.

Never hesitate, said Sergeant Black, so I don't. I fly along the rocky outcrop and shove that pirate hard. His shoulder is warm and firm under my hands, but only for a moment. Because in the next heartbeat he's over the cliff, the box tumbling free and him wildly clawing at air.

He makes a sound as he falls. A yelp, almost. Then there's a dull, wet sound, like a melon dropped on concrete.

My heart is beating in big, shuddery thumps. I force myself to creep to the edge of the cliff, and there at the bottom sprawls the pirate. The chest is in pieces, and there are gold and silver coins all over the sand. He's facedown, his arm bent at an awkward angle, and he's moaning, trying and failing to sit up.

"What—what have you *done*?"

A second pirate is running at me. His beard takes up most of his face, and his hands are already in fists.

They must have taken treasure from the common pile. If

you're a pirate, stealing from your own will get you hanged by your own. Unless you can hide your loot and come back for it later without anyone being the wiser.

You'd want somewhere like the point. It's noteworthy enough that a person who knows where to look could find it again without much trouble. The tide can't reach the topmost stretch of rocky sand, so anything buried there would go undisturbed until someone came to dig it up.

I've seen their faces, I would know where to look, and I've just shoved one of them over a cliff and hurt him bad.

It won't matter if Vivienne sends a boat back for me. There won't be much left of me to find.

I drop to my knees and slide my legs over the side of the cliff. My bare feet scrabble, but there's no toehold. The beardy pirate is clearing the trees, so I shove myself backward and screech as the rocky cliff tears up my legs through Alivarda's trousers. My fingers get chewed to hamburger trying to slow myself down, and I end up falling the last few yards and landing on the pirate I pushed.

He bellows like a dying boar, and I fling myself off him.

At the top of the cliff, his friend is shouting at me in the common language, demanding that I *wait* and *hold on* and other things I ignore. The injured pirate is moaning now, gasping sharp and shallow. There's blood down his forehead and leaking out his ears.

The world is spinning. Famine drop, the newspapers called

it. When your body is trying to function on food that isn't filling. I squint at the ocean and the Ariminthian ship. It looks a little smaller, like it's sailing away. If I couldn't make it before, I definitely can't now.

A few stones tumble past me. The beardy pirate is starting to climb down. He's swearing now, growling like a dog.

There's nowhere to run on this little beach. It's shaped like a crescent moon, and the points jut out like walls into the sea.

I sure as anything can't stay here.

I splash into the water up to my knees. Hoping hard it's shallow so I can wade around one of the points and get to another stretch of beach and back into the jungle. But one tentative step sinks me to my neck and I go stumbling back.

I'm soaking wet, arms crossed tight over my chest because I know how I must look to a pirate who's angry about his injured friend and promised fun.

Use what the land gives you.

I turn back toward the rocky beach. The beardy pirate is halfway down the cliff, fumbling for handholds, cursing louder. There's driftwood everywhere, but nothing that could hold my weight. The shovels are wooden. Ancient and blunt, perfect for moving sand. Less perfect as your only defense against pirates.

Then I notice the lid of the sea chest that the injured pirate was carrying. The one that broke when he fell. It's the size of a gravestone and dark with tar.

I slosh back ashore and grab it, holding it in front of me with both hands. It's sticky and smells like creosote, but I grip it hard and stride back into the water.

"All of you," I whisper to the shushing, endless surf and the island behind me and maybe Vivienne's princess, "please, if you're listening, if you can hear me, help me."

Behind me, there's a crunch that can only be boots hitting sand, and I leap into the water and flail with everything I've got toward that warship.

VIVIENNE

THIS IS WHERE it ends. The island has been waiting for this moment. Toying with me. Now it has whispered to the sea, and the sea will pull me down. I will go soundlessly, my mouth filling with water, just as the princess did.

Then I hear his voice.

Just a little farther, lambkin. Kick those legs! You've got it, like that!

All those days in the harbor, growing stronger, sleek like a porpoise. Me in my little red bathing suit, splashing out to the buoy and back, my father swimming alongside me, treading water till I kept up.

I lift my head and mark the ship. A blur of dark wood and an expanse of pale white sailcloth.

Just a little farther. It always felt possible when he said it.

Stroke on stroke, the royal seal digging into my wrist. I

tied it tight on purpose, so I would not worry that it had fallen off. When my corpse washes up, someone will find it. The princess will make sure that person is Ariminthian, and the seal will find its way to the Royal Mother.

My homeland will survive.

Mama told me to forget about him, and that was easy once enough days had gone by and the princess did not send me back to the scullery. Someone surely must have told her that my father had been sentenced to death for speaking against the war, for attending those meetings in darkened wharfside warehouses, that my very presence in the palace was to work off debts my whole family would owe for at least a generation.

But my mistress never said a word about it. We both let him sink into the sea.

My hand smacks something hard, something that heaves and sways. I look up, and up, swiping water from my eyes.

The ship. I made it. Somehow the sea has let me live.

There now, he'd say once we were at the buoy, *you made it, see? Every stroke brings you closer. One of them brings you there.*

The foredeck towers over me, impossibly high, rolling with the current. There's nothing to hold on to, and the sea still thinks to pull me down. I put two fingers to my mouth and whistle. It's a short, sharp note that brings three sailors quickly. They're wild-eyed and clutching cutlasses, primed for pirate treachery.

"Please. Let me up." I hack it out in Ariminthian.

There's a brief hash of discussion, then a rope net slithers down the side of the ship for me to climb. I'm numb as I go up hand over hand, dripping and half-dressed, and heave myself over the rail and onto the deck in a heap.

All at once, I am small. I am crying. I am dripping wet in my little red bathing suit and watching the gendarmes haul my father away.

He is gone. I am forgetting. I *have* forgotten.

"Blessed ocean—it's a *girl!*"

"She must have escaped the pirates."

"Poor little thing. She looks like a half-drowned kitten."

They're speaking in Ariminthian, and a rush of joy moves through me to hear my own language again. A big sailor helps me up, and a wiry one drops a scratchy wool blanket over my shoulders. A sunburned cabin boy puts a steaming mug of tea in my hands. They've slipped their weapons into their belts, but they still stand battle-ready, poised to strike.

The big sailor holds up both hands to quiet the others, then turns to me. "Who are you? Where did you come from?"

"The island." I sip the tea, and tears jump to my eyes at the warmth of it, the comfort. "I'm a survivor of the *Burying Ground.*"

"Survivor? Oh no. If something happened to it, that's the end of the cease-fire. We're back at war."

"You were on that island? And you *swam* all this way? Honey, why don't you take a seat on this crate?"

"Cap, you'll want to get over here!"

Sailors part, and the captain blows toward me. He comes up close and squints in my face, then turns away with a wince.

The sailors must have told him there was an Ariminthian survivor of the *Burying Ground* who was a girl. The captain was hoping for one of the princesses.

It happens again, like it hasn't in so many days. The height of the waves. The pink of her dress. The raw agony of salt water in my nose, my ears, my throat.

"A servant, then." The captain sighs harshly, but his voice is measured when he asks, "It's true? You were on the *Burying Ground*, and it went down? All the way out here?"

Out of habit, my eyes go right to the ground and stay there. Then I realize he's waiting for an answer, so I nod.

"Filthy Duran—" The captain cuts himself off, then turns to a midshipman. "Tell the gunners to stand down. Come about and beat to windward. Best speed to the capital."

"We're letting pirates *go*?" The midshipman gapes.

"The *Raptor* is now transporting a witness to the greatest maritime disaster in modern history to the palace," the captain says through his teeth. "We have the Durans dead to rights now. There's no way they can keep denying what they've done."

I promised a lifeboat. She had to trust me. I open my mouth, but I am remembering the rules. I am remembering the dim of the chatelaine's cupboard, my fingers helplessly clawing the wood. I am remembering that I am in the presence of my betters.

So I do the only thing I can—lift my arm and point toward the island. Toward Cora, waiting.

The captain is ranting about the *Burying Ground*, how the minister for counterterrorism had been right all along, how the Durans would pay. How there'd be no quarter now, not till Dura was a wasteland.

The midshipman is the one who follows my gesture, squints, then whips a brass spyglass from his belt and snaps it to its full length all in one motion. He nudges the captain and holds out the glass to him, and the captain quiets himself long enough to peer through it before handing it to me.

"What is the meaning of this?" asks the captain in a low, dangerous voice.

I lift the glass to my eye, and Cora comes into wavering focus. She is clinging to the lid of a sea chest while floundering to kick and paddle like an injured sea lion.

"There was another survivor on the island. A Duran girl. That's her." I can speak now. I am within the rules. "Will you send a boat for her?"

The captain takes the spyglass back and puts it to his eye once more. He keeps it there for long, long moments.

"The sea is not always strange," he murmurs. "Sometimes you know exactly what it's doing."

CORA

SOME BLURRY THINGS happen:

An Ariminthian sailor grabs me out of the water by the back of Alivarda's tunic and hauls me into a lifeboat like I'm a swordfish.

The air smells like metal, like smoke, and I am shivering and curled up in the grimy salt water at the bottom of the little boat as it forces its way through the choppy waves.

I am climbing a net made of rope onto an Ariminthian warship.

Then I'm aboard, swaying and dripping water everywhere. There's wood beneath my bare feet and it's solid and it doesn't shift like sand and I'm not on that island anymore.

We've been rescued.

The signal fires worked and we've been *rescued*.

I don't know what to do. Where to stand, where to go. The first and only time I was on a ship was the *Burying Ground*, and there were very specific rules we had to follow that had all been spelled out beforehand as part of the peace agreement.

No. I *do* know what I should do. I should find the captain and tell him everything. Vivienne must have already told him we're survivors of the *Burying Ground*, but maybe she didn't tell him about the treaty.

Or maybe she told him the truth, that the treaty was washed over the side unsigned and now it's gone for good.

Ariminthian sailors crisscross the deck, moving ropes and doing boat things. They don't even glance at me, so I take a few tottering steps toward where I remember the captain's quarters were on the *Burying Ground*, but a sailor steps into my path, slings a thick woolen blanket around me, and steers me to a crate out of the way. He tells me in the common language to *stay put*.

"Can I see the captain?" I ask. "I really need to talk to him."

"Soon. Sit here for now. We must come about and get clear."

I'm too tired to insist. I don't realize how exhausted I am till I'm actually sitting and my legs turn to mush and *I could have drowned*. Vivienne could have left me out there. She could have told the captain to sail away, and I'd have been lucky to make it back to the island and the pirates and the famine drop, waiting for a ship that would likely never come.

I ought to thank her. I'm going to be thanking a lot of Ariminthians in the coming days, and that is not going to be easy, not when I'll be thinking of my brothers every single time.

I guess this is what peace means. Not letting those things go. But putting other things in front of them for the time being.

Sorry, Mom and Dad.

Vivienne must be around here somewhere. The sailors probably whisked her away to a fancy stateroom and gave her dry clothes and meat and gingerbread while I sit here shivering on a crate.

Or maybe not. She's a servant who braids hair, someone who might not even deserve a crate to sit on.

The sailor who brought me the blanket and told me to stay put is leaning against some ropes nearby. He's not threatening or anything, but I get the impression he's been told to watch me.

I guess that makes sense. There might be a cease-fire, but I'm still Duran and this is still an Ariminthian warship.

"Hey." I make myself smile at him. "Where is Vivienne? The other girl?"

"Talking to the captain."

"But you said—" I bite it back. Of course the captain would want to talk to her right away, even with everything else going on. She might be a servant who braids hair, but she's still Ariminthian.

Vivienne told me that her princess hated the war. There's no reason she would want to ruin the cease-fire by telling the captain that the treaty was never signed.

Would she?

I can barely keep still, and it feels like forever before a burly graybeard appears. He's got a blue kerchief around his neck, and his bald spot is shiny amid the white nest of hair curling at his ears.

"This way, Duran," he says. "The captain's ready to speak with you."

The graybeard opens a door that leads into a long, dim passageway lit with hurricane lamps.

Always listen to your gut. If something feels off, it probably is.

Right now my gut is telling me that this is my chance to convince the captain that the treaty was signed before the storm hit. My parents always said that the Ariminthians loved the war, but at least one of them didn't, and her dad was the freaking *king* of Ariminthia.

Vivienne was her friend. Maybe that means Vivienne doesn't like the war, either.

"Duran." The graybeard tips his chin at the hallway. "You don't keep the captain waiting."

I take a deep breath and follow the graybeard down the hall, to the last door at the end. The captain's room is big enough to accommodate a desk covered with papers and a dining table that's been set with real porcelain dishware and metal cutlery on top of a white cloth.

Maybe the captain will invite us to supper. Survivors of the *Burying Ground* will get the best of everything.

Please. Yes. *Please* invite us to supper.

The captain is sitting behind his desk. When I step into the room, he stands up. He's wearing a long blue greatcoat and a patterned vest, and his expression is unreadable.

I remember from the *Burying Ground* that most captains come from the minor gentry, which is an Ariminthian way of saying someone doesn't have noble blood but they're still better than a regular person. Just the idea makes me want to roll my eyes so hard that it might actually hurt my face, but I need to speak to him in a way that will make him listen.

"First I want to thank you." I say it fast, rattling that part out because I want to get it over with. "You saved us. You saw our fires, right? Those were my idea. And they *worked*."

The captain nods but doesn't reply. I wonder how well he understands the common language. Supposedly everyone knows a little, but some people know more than others, and some people pretend not to know much at all because they don't like the idea of it even existing.

"I can't believe I'm going home." I hug myself a little because it still doesn't feel real. "How long will the voyage be, do you think?"

The captain frowns slightly. "The voyage?"

"To the neutral port," I reply. "Vivienne told you, right? How the treaty was signed before that storm hit? The *Burying Ground* was supposed to go to the neutral port, so I know you'll want to sail there straightaway and let everyone know there's peace."

The captain sits down in a creak of leather. "Is that what I want?"

I blink. "Well. Sorry. The common language can be weird sometimes. What I meant to say is that I'm so happy to be rescued, and I can't wait to get home and tell everyone that we have peace now."

His frown deepens, and my face is getting hot, and I can't help but fill the silence with something, *anything*. "I also can't wait to tell everyone what it was like on the island. Vivienne found a bunch of trunks with food in them, but would you believe I had nothing to eat but these purple berries? I have no idea how I survived."

The captain sits up straighter. "You didn't expect to survive, then."

The *Burying Ground* reeled, heaving up and falling hard. Heavy sheets of rain seemed to shatter the deck into toothpicks. The signing table shuddered deep into the mushy planks, and the next pitch of the ship sent it flying into the prime minister and his wife before it sank like a brick into the sea.

My dad grabbed for my hand and missed.

Everything screamed. The wind. The people. Everything.

"N-no. That storm was really bad." I force a chuckle even though my stomach is in knots. "I wish I could tell you more about where we were or what happened, but I honestly don't know anything about ships or wind or navigation or whatever. That's more of a you thing. Maybe Vivienne could tell you, though."

Or maybe not, since servants who braid hair are not allowed to think for themselves. But that's probably not the best thing to say right now to someone whose good side I need to be on.

"On the contrary," the captain replies, "I think there's a lot you can tell me about what happened."

He doesn't say it mean, but there's something about it I don't like. It's not a *minor gentry* thing, either. It's not even a weirdness in the common language.

Something else is going on.

"I just told you what happened. There was a storm."

The captain's face twitches. "*That's* the story you're going with?"

I frown at the word *story*. In my head I translate it into Duran and back into the common language. Then I say, slowly, "It's what happened. But don't worry. The treaty was signed before—"

"The *Burying Ground* was a dreadnought, built with springwood, board by board and joint by joint." His voice is cold. "No mere storm could sink it."

We learned about springwood in school. It only grows on certain islands on the high seas. The Ariminthians build their ships with it because it's lightweight and sturdy and also doesn't get ruined by salt water like other wood, but there's a trick to working with it that the treaty was going to force them to share so we could make ships as strong as theirs. Until we know that, the only good thing about springwood is how you can tell there are minerals in the soil beneath that'll make good mining because springwood trees thrive on them.

"Well." I shift uncomfortably, pulling the blanket tighter. "This wasn't an ordinary storm, believe me. It was . . ."

The sky turned a bad color. A breeze picked up, brisk and

threatening. Some sailors scurried up the masts and took in all the sails, clinging like spiders, while others tied things down on the deck. The captain kept checking his compass, frowning and shaking it like a nursery kid with a broken toy.

Then the wind and rain hit, and the next thing I knew I was in the water, grabbing at whatever I could. Everything wooden turned to splinters in my hands, slick with something like oil. Masts. Planks. Lifeboats and oars.

"I know exactly what it was," this captain snaps. "Everyone knows."

"Wait." I'm scrambling through my memory to that darkened room, to us sitting in a circle, to Sergeant Black's matter-of-fact calm. "Are we still at war?"

"What we don't know is *how*," the captain says quietly. "All those precautions, all that security. All those empty Duran promises. And for what?"

The graybeard is standing in the doorway, arms folded like a guard at a roadside checkpoint.

"Maybe it doesn't matter." The captain laughs humorlessly. "You'll never tell us, will you? None of them do."

"I . . . I don't think I have anything else to say." I'm trembling. Thanking all those martyrs for the Raritan Accords. "I am invoking my rights as a prisoner of war."

The captain stands up so fast that his desk jolts and the pens and inkwells rattle. "Fine. That's as good as a confession to me. Bosun, show this Duran to the brig."

The graybeard steps toward me, but I pull away even though it takes me farther into the captain's room and toward that neatly set table I'm not going to sit at.

"I—I know every word of the Raritan Accords," I stammer. "Prisoners of war can't be tortured. They have to be fed and kept in decent conditions."

"Oh, honey, don't worry." The captain braces both hands on his desk. "Nothing bad will happen to you on my ship."

My gut is crawling now.

"Not when you'll be heading back to Ariminthia to stand trial for war crimes." He narrows his eyes. "For the sinking of the *Burying Ground*."

WAR CRIMES

VIVIENNE

I CANNOT GET Cora's blasphemy out of my head.

Maybe this is why the princess is helping me. Maybe she even wanted me to ruin her shrine.

That would also mean the princess sent the pirates so I would recover the royal seal. It would mean the princess helped Cora survive the storm and washed her up on our island so she would be there to save me from them.

The captain summons me to his quarters. The scratchy sea blanket is still over my shoulders, and I am wavering on unsteady legs and dripping salt water all over his polished floor.

There's a green leather wing chair near the desk, and the captain must notice me glancing at it because he kindly tells me to sit, even though my damp back and bottom will ruin the finish.

"You and the Duran girl were on the island together," he says. "Did she reveal anything to you?"

"Blasphemy," I mutter, which makes the captain chuckle.

"No, honey. Did she tell you how she sank the *Burying Ground*? How she was able to smuggle the components on board? How she kept from being noticed? Who her orders came from?"

I am remembering how my mistress clutched a small ivory turtle in her left hand, rubbing its shell with her thumb. She said it helped her stay in the moment. It helped remind her that at least one thing in the world was solid.

I am remembering how the sea came up and over the deck like it had no idea that my mistress and her family were there. Like it really saw no difference between us and the Durans.

I fight down tears. I am not ashamed to cry for her, but right now that will not help her. It will not help anyone.

The captain must remember who he's talking to, because he adds, "You may speak."

"Much of the time, the Duran girl and I did not interact at all," I reply in my palace voice, eyes on the ground. "It was only when the pirates arrived that we learned of each other's presence."

"And you did not abandon her on the island because you knew she was the saboteur," the captain says. "You wanted her to stand trial for the assassination of the royal family."

He is not asking.

The sea did not deliver the royal seal of Ariminthia to me. The sea delivered it to Cora.

"Perhaps there was a blast," the captain suggests. "Close to the waterline? That would make the ship take on water and go down quickly."

I am remembering the crown prince telling his sisters about the *Burying Ground*, how it was built to exacting standards for the occasion. A forty-gun dreadnought, the mightiest and grandest in the Ariminthian fleet, sturdy enough to withstand the kind of treachery the minister for counterterrorism anticipated.

I am remembering the double ring of gendarmes guarding the ship as we boarded. I watched the bomb-sniffing dogs led over every board twice and thrice before we cast off. No Duran agent could have sneaked on board to plant a bomb while we were in Ariminthia, and after the Duran delegation came aboard at the neutral port, they stayed in plain sight on their side of the foredeck. Just as they agreed to.

I shake my head.

The captain scowls faintly. "If not a blast, then *what*?"

When the wind began in earnest and the sailors went up the rigging, my mistress cowered behind her sisters, and I stood with my shoulder pressed against hers, holding her hand tight and tighter as the deck rolled beneath her new leather boots, and she rubbed her turtle like that simple act was anchoring her to the seafloor fathoms and fathoms below.

"There was a storm," I whisper.

His scowl turns ominous. "Have a care, my girl. It almost sounds like you're suggesting that an Ariminthian dreadnought is unable to withstand a storm."

"No, of course not," I say to my feet.

"Then you will need to think harder," the captain replies. "Whatever happened to the *Burying Ground*, it wasn't just a storm."

Just a storm. That iron latticework table slamming into two Duran functionaries and sending them screaming into the churning surf. A yard with scraps of a sail crushing the crown prince as he hurried his oldest sister toward a lifeboat she never made it to.

I can't take my eyes off the salt water puddling on the floor. A warship captain should know better than to tell the sea what it did and did not do.

"If the ship was sunk because of a blast, the Durans are to blame," the captain adds quietly. "If it was a storm, they are not to blame. We are. We're the ones who built the *Burying Ground* for the peace accords. We're the ones who manned and sailed it."

The minister for counterterrorism personally chose the shipyard, hand-selected the craftsmen, and deployed his own constabulary as a security detail. He inspected every joint and beam as the ship came together. He even commissioned a silversmith to make an ornate compass as a gift for the captain, presented solemnly in the presence of the sea.

I shake my head. I don't want Ariminthia to take the blame.

"We should arrive in the capital in a week's sailing," the captain says. "Plenty of time for you to remember something useful for the trial—and stop repeating this nonsense about a storm."

"Aren't—" I stop myself, because speaking in my palace voice again is reminding me of being small, crouching in corners, doing as I'm told.

"Yes?" The captain seems impatient.

"Aren't you going to stay in the area and look for survivors?"

He shakes his head. "I've noted the location of your island and entered a detailed description in my log. When we return to the capital and I've reported to the lords of the admiralty, they'll send ships to comb this part of the high seas. If there are other survivors, we'll find them. Don't you worry about that."

"Ah." I squirm in my wet clothes. "Wouldn't it be better to find them now? The island made sure I had plenty to eat, but that might not be the case for others."

"No, honey, no. I can't in good conscience do anything but make for home at best speed. A Duran saboteur has murdered the royal family to gain the upper hand, just as we feared they would. That's as clear as anything now."

I want to agree. I want it to be clear. But I saw the sky turn dark. I saw the sea turn against us, all of us, Ariminthian and Duran alike.

"All their talk of peace—hogwash. Just a smoke screen so we'd let our guard down." The captain smiles grimly. "But I'd wager ten gold thalers that the Durans did not expect there to be evidence. They did not expect their saboteur to survive."

The princess was helping Cora. So was the island. There's absolutely no question about that.

There's but one reason my mistress might help a Duran saboteur, especially one who was instrumental in her own demise.

"If there are other survivors, we'll find them as soon as possible, but we only need one to tell the high court what happened to the *Burying Ground*." The captain peers at me carefully. "Do you understand?"

I nod. I do understand.

"Aww, honey, it'll be all right." The captain's manner softens, and he pours me a steaming cup of coffee. "Here. Drink up. You look like you're about to collapse. I'll have the bosun find you some dry clothes and take you down to the sailors' mess for a hot meal. Don't worry about the trial. It'll be over before you know it, and then you'll be back at the palace."

The coffee is sweet and strong, but I don't even taste it.

It must be a silver lining for you. You don't have to be anyone's servant. You can just be a regular kid.

My wrist aches under the blanket where the royal seal is bound tightly, to keep it safe from the restless, inscrutable sea.

This is why I was spared. This and this alone.

My pockets still smell faintly of cockles. The sand from the island collected at the bottom, which not even the sea dared remove.

CORA

"IT'S NOT SUPPOSED to be like this," I whisper to the dank, dripping walls, to the slant of pale daylight that slinks through the porthole.

We are not on our way to the neutral port. The captain didn't even care about the treaty, signed or otherwise.

No medals. No meeting with the prime minister. No reporters.

Instead I'm going to be tried for war crimes. *War crimes*. I still have stuffed toys in my bed.

The brig isn't quite two paces wide and barely tall enough for me to stand up in. It's clearly made for someone much larger than me, a big sailor who would have to stoop and crouch, which is likely part of the punishment. All I can hear is the grumbling creak of the hull beneath my feet, which are slopping around in something I sure hope is water.

My clothes are drying on me, clammy and damp, and I'm

starting to get chilly. Alivarda's clothes, I should say. They took his knife when they searched me, as if that tiny dull blade would do me any good here.

"They'll have to follow the Raritan Accords at least," I say to Alivarda. "That means there'll have to be a judge and a jury and actual *evidence*, which they don't have. They can't just *decide* I'm guilty."

Can they?

I'm not good at sitting still. When I woke up on the island, alone and in my underwear, at least there were things I could do. Some of them weren't very smart, but at least I could be *doing*.

Here in the brig, though, the only thing to do is watch the barred brick of sunlight from the porthole disappear as the morning wears on, and wait for the grizzled old sailor who brings a helping of lukewarm stew in a dented mug three times a day.

I plan ways I could escape. Overpower that old man and rush upstairs, where in my little fantasy world I also overpower the captain and have half a clue how to steer a ship, so I sail myself back to Dura, where I assure both Parliament and the newspapers that the treaty was signed and there's peace now and it's all because of me.

I'm watching a bead of water dribble down the wall when there's a soft pattering of footsteps, and Vivienne appears outside my cell. She's scrubbed clean of mud—*lucky*—and wearing a cabin boy's tunic and trousers that are much too big, hanging well past her wrists and rolled at the ankles.

We are still at war. My first priority is survival.

But we were weeks in the jungle, she and I. The signal fires may have been my idea, but without her bowl and those cockles, the famine drop would have slowed us both down enough to be easy prey for pirates. She'd have been eaten alive by bugs had she not rubbed herself with mud like I told her, and I'd still be rotting on the island or drowned had she not gotten the captain to send a lifeboat.

During those weeks, we had a cease-fire.

"I'm not supposed to be down here," Vivienne says importantly. "I decided to come. On my own."

I fight a scowl. What does she want, a freaking medal?

"I figured out why my mistress was helping you on the island. She wanted you to stay alive long enough for us to find you. She wanted you to have a reason to come aboard an Ariminthian ship. She wants you to face justice."

I meet Vivienne's eyes steady on. "I see. This is payback. You're still mad that I ruined that shrine, so you told the captain that I sank the *Burying Ground*."

"I—I did *not*. I told him *nothing*." She's ruffled, almost indignant, but then she mutters, "He did not want to listen to me anyway."

I snort. That at least feels familiar.

"He decided I was guilty before I said a word," I grumble. "It doesn't even make sense! Why would I do something like that? Why would *anyone*?"

"To win the war," she replies simply. "You weren't going to win it any other way."

"But that—that—Are you really saying I might sink a ship that my own parents were on—that *I myself with my own body* was on—just to win the war? How would that even be possible?"

"I imagine your government thought murdering the royal family would destabilize Ariminthia and start a civil war," Vivienne says. "Then with our navy in disarray, you'd use your machines to invade once and for all."

"Okay. All right." I pace my tiny cage twice before returning to the bars. "That is a *ridiculous* thing to think. Dura would be messed up, too! There would have to be special elections and emergency powers, and Parliament would need to—"

I stop, because I don't even *know* what Parliament would need to do. Who would be in charge. How they would even decide.

Finally I manage, "Who in their right mind could possibly think sinking a ship on purpose that was carrying the whole peace delegation was a good idea?"

Vivienne crosses her arms. "You were probably ordered to. Considering you were *trained*."

It takes a moment. Two or three moments. But oh. I did snap it at her, there on the sand when we'd run from the pirates, when I was sure they'd catch us if I wasn't calling the shots.

I am in enough trouble without anything that sounds even remotely like a confession, but I can't help it. I laugh aloud.

"*Trained?* A bunch of twelve-year-olds in invasion readiness training learning to disguise their footprints and make a shelter with a bedsheet? *That's* who you think sunk the *Burying Ground*? My parents won't even let me wear a skirt without tights!"

Vivienne bites her lip. Even in the faint light, she seems to pale. "Then it's true? That's what you called it?"

"It's—what are you even talking about right now?"

"Invasion readiness training," Vivienne whispers. "The secret Duran military training program for children. The one readying you to invade."

"What? No!" I grip the bars. "We had to learn what to do if your lot invaded *us*!"

"That's what they told you?" She sounds almost pitying. "If we could invade Dura by land and end the war, we'd have done it long ago. The only reason the war's still going on is your machines keep bombarding our cities with incendiaries, and your saboteurs keep attacking supply depots and bridges and hospitals."

I don't even dignify that with a response. The reason the war is still going on is because the Ariminthians keep destroying Duran mining outposts on islands that are in neutral waters and murdering the crews. Ariminthia might have better ships, but that doesn't mean they get to decide what happens with every square inch of ground that pokes out of the ocean.

"All right. All right." I make myself stay calm. "If the princess can do stuff like help me even though she's dead, why didn't she stop the *Burying Ground* from sinking in the first place?"

"The sea is strange," Vivienne replies serenely. "Its ways

are not for us to know, and all we can do is make offerings and ask for its blessings. Once the sea decided to take the *Burying Ground*, nothing could stop it. But once the sea claimed my mistress, she was in a position to do things."

"Are you sure the princess is the one who wants justice? Or is it *you*?"

Vivienne's eyes widen. All at once I'm glad for the bars because I bet she's still got that piece of twine on her somewhere.

"What I mean is, you said on the island that your princess didn't like the war," I go on quickly. "Do you really think that someone who wanted peace would want me tried for war crimes? Parliament is going to *freak out* if that happens, especially if I'm convicted. Things will get way worse."

"There's no other explanation, though," Vivienne whispers. "It had to be sabotage, and you're the only Duran on board who was the right age."

"*Had* to be? *Why*, though?" I fight to keep my voice even. "Viv, you were *there*. It was a storm. You saw it same as me. A storm that was bad enough to smash that ship to pieces."

She sighs impatiently. "Durans vote for their leaders, yes? If you didn't like the war, you would vote for someone who would make peace."

"Well. It doesn't work like that." I frown and try again. "I mean, yes, that's how it's supposed to work. But it's unpatriotic to be against the war, so no one would ever run on a peace platform. They'd never be elected."

"Then if you don't like the war, and you can't vote for someone to end the war because no one against the war is allowed to govern, how is that different from having a lord?"

"I . . ." I flounder is what I do. Vivienne waits, but I don't answer because it's complicated and the way she says it makes it sound so simple.

"That is why it must be sabotage," she says at last. "Your leaders have no intention of making peace, or they'd have done so by now, because Durans would have chosen leaders who would."

"Well." I fluster myself into order. "The same is true for yours, then. Only without the choosing part. My dad always says that the Ariminthian nobility will fight to the last peasant before they'll admit defeat."

She scowls, and I rush on, "All I mean is that it doesn't *have* to be sabotage just because the captain says so. He wasn't there. We were! I just . . . my *parents* were on that ship! You have something to go back to. It sucks that you lost your princess, but you can braid someone else's hair. I'm a freaking *orphan* now!"

Vivienne flinches like I hit her, and for half an instant I feel bad, but then I bloody well don't.

Because oh. I just said it out loud. I'm an orphan now.

"Look. All right. That was mean, and I shouldn't have said it." I'm talking fast because I can only fight one war at a time. "But I have an idea. You're going back to the palace once we land in Ariminthia, right? What if I could talk to the king? The new king, I mean. You could get him to, I don't know, *summon* me, and then we could tell him together what happened to the *Burying Ground*. The truth, that it was a storm. Then he could send a message to Parliament and we could tell them. If everyone knows what happened, that it was no one's fault *and* that the treaty was already signed—maybe there could be peace."

Vivienne edges a step back. "You are . . . assuming a lot about what I can and cannot do."

I slump onto my bench like a dishrag. All at once I'm wondering if I've been assuming a lot about what *I* can do, as well. If there were ever going to be meetings with Parliament and medals and state dinners. If there were going to be reporters and lead stories and a nice, shiny spotlight.

"Do you even *want* peace?" I whisper. "You. Vivienne. Not your princess. *You.*"

Vivienne looks down. She starts fidgeting with some hidden thing at her wrist that's under the cuff of her tunic.

She doesn't answer and she doesn't answer. Finally she mumbles something about wanting, something about the sea.

Then she's up the corridor, soundless like a shadow, leaving me alone in the dim.

VIVIENNE

THE BOSUN SHOWS me to his quarters and tells me I'll be staying there on the voyage home while he sleeps before the mast with the sailors. It's too much for someone like me, and I tell him so.

He says it's captain's orders. Only the best for a survivor of the *Burying Ground*, soon to be the star witness in the war crimes trial.

I shift a little, like my clothes are still full of sand.

It's not very late, but I'm exhausted. In the bosun's quarters, there's a hammock strung on two sturdy hooks, corner to corner like you do in a modest space, and in that moment where the air smells of brine and there's a wind through hemp and canvas, I'm small again and I'm in a hammock like this one, and there's a soft fan of candlelight overhead and my mother and father are singing a hauling song to get me to sleep, and my father's big rough hand is gently sending the hammock into motion while their voices echo in that little cozy house by the wharf.

Cora said I had something to go back to. That I could braid someone else's hair, as if that is something I could just decide.

My mistress had not wanted a lady's maid. She wanted her childhood nurse to stay forever, but her fathers insisted. It was time to grow up, the king told her, and this time her other father did not dispute him.

The older princesses each had maids who came from the gentry, ambitious girls who intended to make the most of royal connections. My mistress was twelve, already the subject of whispers. Despite very attractive incentives, only two girls expressed an interest in the role. The first lasted three months; the second just a week. After word got around, not even ambition could make another daughter of the gentry come near her.

The king and his consort must have known there'd be no one else but me to be her maid. Perhaps they considered it more remunerative than the scullery.

In this hammock on the *Raptor*, I sleep hard and dreamless, rocked by the sea.

As we sail toward Ariminthia, I have no duties to fill my time. It's a bit like those days on the island, nothing to do but set fires where I thought best and dig cockles in warm, smooth sand, but here there is no constant drumbeat of fear, looking over my shoulder for pirates, flinching at every twig snap.

Here, I take the salt air. I lean on the rail. I watch the crew at work and overhear their muttered gossip. It might be dated, but that does not stop them from worrying it like a loosened scab.

Can't say I'm looking forward to getting back. The whole city's on edge.

Think how bad it'll be once folks hear the news.

Good thing the palace thought to recall the king's brothers from the front, just in case. We can't be without a king. Not if Dura's coming for us.

Where are the king's brothers, though? Seems like it's one delay after another.

The noble lords were gathering even before we sailed. They think something's in the wind. You know what? I agree with them.

The trial and execution are sure to steady things some. No one will dare challenge what's got to happen next.

I think about Cora, down in the brig. I wonder if she knows that her fate is sealed, that the high court will not need evidence to convict her.

That she *is* the evidence.

The captain invites me to stand on the foredeck with him to watch Ariminthia appear over the horizon and smudge its way into view. A cabin boy brings the messenger birds in their cages, and once the captain's missives are secured to their legs, they're loosed in a flutter and disappear toward shore.

It's a beautiful blue day, the wind at our back, and there is a small treacherous part of me that swells with unrelenting joy to see my homeland again, even without the princess.

Even knowing my task is almost complete and my own fate awaits.

"We made good time," the captain says. "I've let the admiralty know we're coming. They'll make all the necessary arrangements. Once we've transported the prisoner to the gatehouse, I'll see to it that you're escorted safely where you need to go."

This is what I was meant to do. Beginning with the sea pushing me onto that island, to the island providing wood for signal fires and cockles to keep breath in body. I will kneel before the Royal Mother and present the seal. She will take it and rule.

I will be left to my turnips and my dark corners till I'm too old to lift a knife and I am given to the sea.

The wharves grow ever nearer, stretching around the capital like a second city. Tall masts of ships sway and bob, sway and bob, while sailors and dockworkers heave and haul and trundle under every kind of cargo. I breathe in the brine and close my eyes.

I am *home*.

Warships usually anchor on the eastern side of the harbor, near the admiralty and the shanty district packed with brothels and alehouses. The *Raptor* is heading straight for the city center, which means we're bound for Tideland Dock.

The row of steel cages stretches into the harbor like a breakwater, and as we near, I can make out criminals in different stages of reclamation. Two are rotting already, seabirds picking at their corpses, while three others are still alive, having climbed to the topmost bars to keep their heads above water during high tide.

The tidal cages are not for the ordinary run of cutpurses and murderers. That lot are bound for the galleys or the brothels, where their labor can be put to use until they're used up, and then they will feed the sea.

The cages are for anyone who stands against the war, and therefore against Ariminthia. The sea is allowed to claim them in whatever way it wishes, in whatever time it sees fit.

It's where my father must have spent his final days, all those years ago when they took him away.

It's where Cora will be within a fortnight.

The captain gives an order, and the anchor rumbles from the chain locker and drags us to a stop. Around us, sailors haul lines and trim sails while the bosun fusses with the ship's boat and has it lowered over the side.

You have something to go back to.

But what I think of is the island, even without the princess or her shrine. Those days when I woke up and had only myself to think of, when I could choose this beach or that one to set a signal fire. When I filled that silver bowl with cockles with my own hands till they spilled over, not because anyone told me to but because it needed doing.

"Hey! Let *go* of me! What do you think I'm gonna do, *run*? I don't even know where I am!"

I turn, and Cora is struggling against two marines who have her by each arm. She is squinting against the daylight after all that time in the dim of the brig. She looks dirty and scared and, if possible, in even worse condition than she was on the island.

Cora blinks and blinks and then falls still. She is taking in the vastness of the harbor, the field of boats and ships, the batteries on the hillsides packed with cannon, the glittering city that stretches beyond, out to the horizon and out of sight.

"Crackers," she murmurs. "This is really happening."

She turns to me then, as if she expects me to do something. The starkness of her fear is chilling.

It's unlikely that a Duran ship would have found us and picked us up, but not impossible.

I could be standing where she is right now.

"She doesn't leave your sight from now on," the captain tells the marines in Ariminthian.

"Suicide watch?" the brawny marine asks, and the captain nods grimly.

"Captain, hey!" Cora waves for his attention. "It's stupid for your king to kill me when he could *ransom* me. The Duran Parliament would pay a mint to get me back."

"Can we gag her?" the brawny marine asks the captain in the common language. "I don't want to have to listen to this nonsense all the way to the gatehouse."

"I say we just stick her in the cages now," the other marine mutters.

"Where are you taking me? You have to tell me, you know." Cora glares furiously at first one marine and then the other. "It's in the Raritan Accords."

I know little of the accords, only that they were passed years ago after a public massacre of prisoners of war followed by a retaliatory massacre twice as gruesome. Cora seems convinced they'll be the saving of her. That there can ever be fairness when it comes to war.

The captain sighs. "Very well. For all the good it will do you, here is the information to which you are entitled by way of the Raritan Accords: You are being held on the charge of war crimes, namely, the sinking of the *Burying Ground* and the assassination of the entire Ariminthian royal family. You will be held at the Tideland Dock gatehouse until your trial, and when you are convicted, you will be sentenced to death by way of the tidal cages."

He gestures at the row of gleaming steel, the human wrecks within, and Cora's eyes grow huge.

"Wait. Wait." She swallows hard. "You said *when*. *When* I am convicted. Are you saying that I won't get a fair trial?"

The marines begin to snicker. They are young men, each over six feet, the kind of boy the older princesses would have tossed flowers to in a parade.

Cora is trying not to panic. After so many years of seeing that same look about my mistress, I know it well.

She glances at me again, but just for a moment. Just long enough that I see her disappointment.

I don't know what she'd have me do. Even if I wasn't returning to the palace, there's precious little anyone can do for her now.

"So it's true what they say about Ariminthians, then?" Cora turns her fury on the captain. "Can't pass up a chance to keep the war going, can you? Even you *minor gentry* toolbags love it too much. You love getting peasants killed for your own glory too much. You—"

"Lads, take her away." The captain gestures to the marines, who are more than happy to drag Cora across the deck toward the ship's boat. She goes fighting and squalling that they are *warmongers* and *dillholes* and a lot of words in Duran that are probably much worse.

If she didn't know her fate before, she does now.

"Ugh." The captain curls his lip. "You hear rumors. Then you *encounter* one of them."

Cora goes on and on, shouting, violent, loud, all the way to the rail, and she keeps going even once they've manhandled her over the side. She doesn't once beg for her life. She doesn't whimper or plead.

Despite her noise being mostly blasphemy, it's the most Ariminthian thing I've ever seen her do.

"I thought perhaps the trial would be tricky, given how young she is, but the moment she opens her mouth—" The captain laughs. "Well. Come with me, my girl. I see that the bosun has readied the other boat. They'll be expecting us at the admiralty."

"Not the palace?" It does not come out in my palace voice.

"The lords of the admiralty will want to hear what you have to say so they can better prepare for the trial," the captain explains, as if there's any outcome but the one.

They want to hear what I have to say, as long as I say the things they want to hear.

"How long will it take?" I twist the royal seal around my wrist under the cuff of my tunic.

I hope it takes ten minutes. I hope it takes forever.

The captain frowns. "It takes as long as it takes."

"Yes, my lord. Only . . ." If the sailors are right, if the city is on edge because there's something in the wind, there's no time to lose. I can't spare the noble lords of the admiralty a single moment. Not until the Royal Mother has the seal and the realm is safe.

"Only *what*?" the captain growls.

But even as he says it, a long, graceful barge comes into view. It's painted royal crimson, easy to mark as it glides through the water with each pull of the oars.

The captain swears aloud even as a chill goes down my back.

The princess has sent the royal barge. She is telling me to leave the island behind. She is telling me to do my duty by Ariminthia whatever the cost, just as she did.

She is telling me to hurry.

CORA

I HATE TO admit it, but Ariminthia is beautiful.

When I went to school, we read newspaper articles that described our enemy's towns as peeling and salt-ravaged and dumpy, crammed with shacks that cling to bleak stretches of dirty gravel. We learned that the king cares little for his subjects and makes them pay taxes so he can live in a marble palace while they struggle to stay fed.

But the city I'm being rowed toward is full of tall sleek buildings that are painted bright colors. The docks are sturdy and well made, with only the faintest scruff of weathering and algae. Many windows catch light and wink, which means they have glass panes and they're not that cheap stuff that's as thick as your finger and full of bubbles.

The water is the most beautiful, clean, depthless blue, which

I know because I'm considering throwing myself over the side of this little boat and sinking to the bottom and cheating the hangman.

Only these warmongers would pull me out and give me mouth-to-mouth, and then I'd be grossed out touching lips with an Ariminthian and also soaking wet.

Also, there is no hangman. Just those cages I can't quite bring myself to look at.

Vivienne was never going to be any help. I keep trying to remember something useful from training, but we learned precious little about what to do if we were captured beyond keep our mouths shut.

As if the sergeants didn't think it would matter.

The wharf we're rowing toward is lined with men in blue jackets. They're holding rifles, and there's a low roaring that rises steadily over the ocean's mellow *shush*. For all their bold talk, the marines didn't gag me or even bind my wrists, so when one of them gestures to the slimy ladder, I steady myself and start climbing.

At the top of the ladder, I stop short. There's a massive crowd at the head of the dock. A series of sturdy longshoremen hold ropes like a barrier, and there are soldiers keeping a surge of people behind it.

The crowd is yelling things, mostly in Ariminthian but also in the common language. This is how I know they want me dead.

Not just dead. Violently, *graphically* dead.

There's a wagon there, too, in the midst of the crowd. It's

not an ordinary wagon—it's a solid box on wheels with only one small barred window. The wheels are massive, and the whole thing rides low to the ground, probably to make it hard to tip over. Two huge horses stand in the traces, and there's a hooded figure all in black on the driver's seat holding the reins.

"Let's go," snaps one of the marines, and he grabs my arm and hauls me forward, up the dock.

Somehow I make myself keep up.

The dock isn't long, perhaps a stone's throw, but it stretches out and out like a ribbon unfurling. My breath rattles in my ears, and the marines' grip on my arms is the only thing making me move. As we near the wagon, the soldiers keeping the crowd at bay force them back another few steps, away from the rear hatch, which stands open.

The marines hoist me up like a stray dog, heave me inside, and push the hatch doors closed with a resounding clatter. The world goes dark but for the stripes of barred daylight high above.

Outside, there's the grating of a metal latch bar and also the snap of a lock. The crowd's bawling is dimmer now, but no less violent.

I make myself breathe.

The wagon jolts into motion, steady and swaying but slow. The marines must be clearing the road ahead of it foot by foot, because the crowd noise is still as strong as ever, but there's nothing in the way.

"Well, I guess this is it," I say aloud, to Sergeant Bale, to my parents, to the ache in the pit of my stomach. There's nothing in the Raritan Accords that says that the trial has to be any certain length, so by the time the Duran government hears what happened to me, I'll be bird food. Even if Parliament wanted to intervene, there's no legal way they can stop the trial or influence the outcome.

They'd have to mount an offensive. At best it would be costly. At worst it would be costly and fail.

I force a chuckle. "This is *not* how I wanted to be in all the newspapers."

All at once, there's a deafening *boom* and the very ground shakes. The horses scream and the wagon is jerked forward at the same time it's shoved from the side, rocking perilously and—after what seems like moments and days and years—landing upright on its wheels with a massive jarring crash.

The crowd's angry bawling turns to screams, and there's a chaos of footfalls and wailing and shouting from every side.

The barred window is too high for me to see out of, even if I jump. I try anyway, but all I can see is a slash of sky and the sharp edge of a building.

The wagon driver shouts something about the horses being loose. The air takes on a bitter smell, acrid like the smoke that pours out of foundries and smithies back home.

"Hey!" I pound furiously on the rear hatch. If the Ariminthians want to watch me drown in a cage, they probably shouldn't let me die in what is almost certainly a fire.

Something lands on the roof with a muffled thud. I turn around in time to see the blade of an ax chop through the boards, then wiggle free and disappear. I yelp and throw myself against the wall.

There's shuffling movement above me, and a dull rumble of urgent voices that I can't make out above the panic of the crowd. The ax blade comes down again and again. Slivers of daylight appear along the boards, and I realize that the roof is pretty thin compared to the walls and rear hatch.

"Hey, you in there!" someone shouts. "Get to the front, all right?"

I barely have time to do it before a scarred hobnail boot comes crashing through the roof, splintering boards like rain. A dense push of smoke follows, and I cough as the ax and boot widen the hole with strong, determined blows.

"That'll do it. Give us that ladder, quick."

It's a girl's voice, and I'd swear it's familiar, but Vivienne is the only girl I know within a month's worth of sailing, and it's definitely not her.

By now it's clear that the crowd outside is panicking hard, out of control, but the voice on the roof is calm and confident. There's another thumping of steps above my head, then a rope ladder slithers through the hole.

"Be quick down there," the girl calls. "The gendarmes are on their way by now, and we need to make the safe house while there's still confusion."

That's Duran she's speaking.

I *do* know that voice. But it can't be her. Not here.

I grab the swaying ladder and climb. It occurs to me that

it may be a trap, but whoever these people are, they're risking being slaughtered by big Ariminthian marines to get me out.

Besides, at the end of this wagon ride is a show trial and certain horrifying death. At this point, I have very little to lose.

The moment I stick my head and shoulders out of the hole, I cough again, hard, because the air is full of thick, cloying smoke that is definitely not normal fire smoke.

That's because a whole block of buildings up the street is charred rubble.

Foundation stones lie strewn across the cobbles, and timbers are scattered into toothpicks over the road. Some people are running and screaming while others lie in still heaps, and the soldiers who were trying to contain the crowd are kneeling next to the injured and trying to free people from collapsed buildings and directing others to safety.

"Crackers," I whisper, but I don't have time for much more, because there's a strong hand on my arm both urging and helping me up and out of the hole. I come struggling, belly-down over the broken planks and wincing away from the jagged edges, then onto my feet where I come face-to-face with—

"Kess?" I manage, because beyond all conceivable belief, here she is, the one kid in invasion readiness training who could lift more and throw farther, who outmaneuvered me in the wilderness drop. She's taller now and her face is all angles and her messy brown hair has been shaved to nubs, but it's the show-off of our training company. It's *Kess*.

She laughs. "Man, haven't heard that name in a while!"

Then she peers into my face and gapes. "Holy crap—*Cordwood*. It's *you*!"

Even here, in the capital city of Dura's sworn enemy, surrounded by smoke from what is very clearly an explosion of some kind, people screaming and bleeding out and rushing for safety—even here, I kind of want to punch her when I hear that stupid, *stupid* nickname.

"We've got to go," says a boy at the other end of the wagon. He's about our age and his head is shaved as well, and he's wearing a battered jacket and carrying a long gun that all at once I can't take my eyes off of.

Kess paws my shoulder like we're old friends. "You're okay, right? You can move? Because we've gotta move."

Another boy has pulled the rope ladder out of the hole, and now he's flinging it over the side of the wagon. Once it's secure, he climbs down, and the first boy tosses the gun to him before following. They both look up expectantly, and Kess nudges me toward the ladder.

My hands are remarkably steady as I go down. The boys hold the dancing rope, and soon I'm on the ground next to them. Kess is beside me a few moments later, and she takes in the scene around her with a brisk, almost businesslike squint.

"Safe house Magnolia," she tells them. "Standard protocol. Go."

Without another word, the boys split apart and head in two different directions, disappearing into the screaming and the shouting and the smoke.

"What is—" I cough again. "What's going on? Kess? How are you here?"

"This is a rescue, Cordwood. I'm here because you need rescuing."

While she speaks, she pulls me across the street, into an alley, and around a corner. The alley is lined with low stone walls that border little gardens. One has a washing line, and Kess is over the fence and back with a pink dress and a flowered scarf.

"Here, put this on over your clothes," she says. "Hike up your pants if you can. Cover your hair. Fast, okay? Actually, do it while we go."

If I had any doubts that this is indeed Kess, they just flew away. I'd know that pushy high-handedness anywhere. Still, I hurry after her, shimmying into the dress, hopping on one foot as I tug the trousers above my knees, and cinching the scarf over my stringy hair.

"Use what the land gives you, right?" she says over her shoulder with a cheerful grin.

It's like going back in time, each of us racing to tie a knot or gather kindling, her always, *always* just a beat ahead of me, Sergeant Bale holding up his big hand to her for a high five.

At the end of the alley, Kess peels off her long overcoat and turns it inside out. The inside is black and nondescript, not blue and covered in buckles, so when she puts it back on, she looks completely different.

She takes in my haphazard outfit, then claps my shoulder again. "You're going to be okay. You need to follow me and look normal. I'm taking you to a safe house. We're going to go quick, but we don't want to draw attention. Understand?"

My head is already aching from the smoke, but I move with her into the road, where we join a stream of people hurrying into the middle of the city, away from the blast. I stop abruptly—we're sure to be caught—but Kess pulls me into motion, and all at once I get it.

We're blending in. We're hiding in plain sight. Me in this grandma dress and her in that coat.

Two blocks later, Kess pulls me into another alley, and we dogleg a few streets up and over before emerging onto another, less crowded road. She walks with a calm I don't feel, but I try to match it.

Only this morning I was bound for the tidal cages for war crimes. Now I'm walking free through the streets of the Ariminthian capital with a kid I haven't seen since I was twelve, who moved away right after training and who I wasn't exactly sorry to see the back of.

"Hoo boy!" Kess laughs low, and it's half a cough. "That went way better than I expected, but they're sure to have checkpoints up by now. If we run into one, let me do the talking, okay? My Ariminthian's pretty good."

None of this feels real. But Kess said this is a rescue, and she might be a show-off but she can't lie to save her life.

Kess leads. I follow. Street by street, alley by alley. Slowly it's sinking in. I'm not going to be tried for war crimes. I'm not going to die in the tidal cages.

I'm going to be okay.

After what feels like ages, she cuts through a dirt yard and stops in front of an unremarkable back door. We're in a neighborhood where the houses are built in a long row, sharing walls and backing to a common alley. If it was brickwork instead of shiplap, it might be our hometown. She knocks in a complicated pattern, and inside four different locks scrape open, revealing a gap that she pushes me through before following herself.

I'm in a kitchen. It's dark in here, and musty. The faded curtains are tightly drawn, and there's no fire in the old-fashioned open hearth. The boy who held the long gun during the smashing of the prison wagon is securing the locks behind us.

"King went to do the standard checks," he says.

Kess nods. "Good. I'll get her settled, then I'll go let Command know the operation was a success. Do we have a butcher's bill?"

"Over sixty killed in the blast," the boy replies. "Those are the reported casualties, anyway. And they are *furious* that she escaped."

Kess laughs and shoulder-bumps the boy. "Rook, my man. Never doubt me."

"We're not done yet," Rook replies. "We've still got to get her out of here, when every soldier, sailor, marine, and gendarme is going to be turning the city upside down to find her."

They're going to get me out of here. It's like being wrapped in a warm blanket after being caught in the rain. I could hug them both, even Rook, who I don't know. Even Kess, who always outshone me.

But something isn't right. Dura is a month away from Ariminthia by water with good winds and no problems. It's been over a week since the *Raptor* found us on the island, and it arrived here *this morning*. Even if they'd known a Duran was on board, Parliament couldn't have sent a rescue team in time.

"We'll just blow the crap out of something else," Kess says, offhand.

"Another blast won't work," Rook warns. "Those roadblocks aren't coming down till they find her. They'll go house to house by nightfall if she isn't turned in or caught at a checkpoint."

"How did you know, though?" I ask, and both of them turn to look at me like they'd forgotten I was here. "That I was in the wagon?"

"To be fair, we didn't know it was *you*. Intel doesn't work that way." Kess darts the briefest glance at Rook. "What we did know was that a Duran survivor of the *Burying Ground* was currently in Ariminthian custody, and that was not going to stand, Cordwood. Not on chess team's watch."

"Don't freaking *call* me that!" It's out of my mouth before I can stop it, and once again I'm finishing a length behind her in yet another footrace and watching her win yet another ribbon for arm-wrestling back when we were kids in invasion readiness training.

The secret Duran military training program for children. The one readying you to invade.

No. No. We learned how to make fires. How to know which

mushrooms wouldn't kill us. Not how to blow the crap out of things and handle a long gun.

"All right. Sorry. Old habits." Kess grins. "No hard feelings, though, right? You almost had me in the wilderness drop."

She gestures to herself, up and down, from her heavy boots to her reversible jacket.

My mouth is sawdust. It's all I can do to whisper, "What do you mean?"

Kess turns to Rook, and he shrugs. "She's going to be debriefed anyway. Tell her if you want."

"Best time in the drop gets recruited into covert operations," she says. "If they like you and you like them—and you can make it through basic training—then you go right into the field. This is war work, this is."

She waggles her gloved hands at me.

I slump hard against the counter. Cold to the marrow.

All that time I spent trying to be the best. All that advice Sergeant Bale had for us. All of it, for one reason.

To find kids who had both the head and stomach for *covert operations*.

Vivienne was right.

"You . . . you moved away," I whisper, but it's dawning on me that wasn't the whole story. She went to basic training, and they taught her how to handle explosives and speak Ariminthian so she could come here and blend in and blow up whole city blocks.

So she'd be on hand to smash open armored wagons and pull out valuable prisoners.

"And became Knight of chess team," Kess replies cheerfully. "I wanted to be Rook, but that name was already taken, and there was no way I was going to be Pawn. Or Queen."

The only reason the war's still going on is your saboteurs keep attacking supply depots and bridges and hospitals.

"So you . . . what, do terrorism? Kill regular people?" My knees feel mushy. "That doesn't sound much like war."

She lifts her brows. "Not to hear guys like your dad tell it."

"You were gonna get her settled," Rook cuts in, casually putting himself between Kess and me. "I bet she's hungry, too. Maybe you should, you know, find her something to eat?"

Kess slaps her forehead in an overdramatic way. "Cordwood! I suck. Sorry! Hey, come with me. We've got a cot set up in here, and Rook will make you a sandwich."

Rook gives her the finger but kneels to open a small icebox in the corner. Kess leads me down the hall and into a small bedroom—dark, curtains pulled—and sure enough, there's a cot and a pile of folded blankets.

"Just sit tight, okay?" Kess is halfway out the door already. "We'll know more soon about how we'll get you home."

I thank her and pull off the housewife dress and sink onto the cot, but I'm trembling too much to relax.

Vivienne was *right*.

This was what invasion readiness training was for.

"*Where is she?*" A new voice, a boy's, spitting fury, coming from the kitchen. The walls are paper-thin, and Kess didn't close the door all the way.

"She's safe, King, what's this—owww! What the hell was that for?"

There's a crash and a clatter, and I'm off the cot and peeking through the crack in the door. I can just see slivers of the kitchen, where Rook is standing between Kess and the other boy from the rescue, an empty plate still in Rook's hand as he hisses at them both to shut up.

"Goddamnit, Knight!" King whisper-shouts. "You *lied* to us. Command is furious. *I* am freaking furious!"

Kess holds her hands out like he's an angry dog. "What were we going to do? Let a Duran survivor of the *Burying Ground* die horribly for the amusement of these shitbirds?"

"Yes!" King snaps. "That is exactly what we should have done! Those are the official orders Command has from Parliament— which I just learned when I went to report the *success* of our freaking mission!"

"Hold on." Rook pivots to face Kess. "You said Command called an audible here. That they got intel about the survivor and decided to extract first and report later."

King barks a laugh. "Ha-ha. No. There was a red envelope. The CO showed it to me."

I've known Kess since we were small. I have never seen her at a loss for words. But she is now, in that dim little kitchen with her lips pressed together, looking like someone is hollowing out her guts with a melon baller.

"So yes, there *were* orders," King goes on, snapping off each word, crisp and angry. "Parliament sent them as a contingency plan before the *Burying Ground* ever sailed."

Rook is pressing a hand against his mouth. Shaking his head slowly, slowly, like he's watching a horse drown in mud.

"This is all *red envelope* stuff, Knight," King growls. "Nowhere near your security clearance or mine. But somehow you knew enough to plan all this out and freaking *lie* to us, which means you also must have known about the order specifically forbidding extraction of any potential survivors."

"Of course we had to extract!" Kess is recovering. "A civilian facing a war crimes charge? In the *closed* Ariminthian high court? When we know exactly what the outcome *and* the punishment will be? I don't know what the hell Parliament is thinking, but they're wrong on this."

"No. They're absolutely right." King's face is growing redder by the moment. "We *should* have let the Ariminthians make a catastrophic error in judgment and gruesomely execute a Duran civilian for something they had *no evidence at all* that she even did. Think how that would look on the front page of every newspaper in Dura. People would be seeing red. There'd be no more of this antiwar crap, and the Defense of Liberty Emergency Powers Act would *sail* through Parliament, and those losers in Embrace Piss could be put in prison where they belong!"

Kess shrugs, but she folds her arms in front of her like a shield. "It was the right thing to do."

"Dude, it doesn't matter!" King replies through his teeth.

"You told us we'd been ordered to rescue her. We did it. But that was not in fact what we were ordered to do, and now we are going to have to answer for having done it." He snorts. "Check that. *You* are going to have to answer for having done it. The CO is on his way here. He's gonna take her into custody."

I stumble away from the door. I sink onto the cot. I lower my head into my hands.

The Kess I know will do something. She'll insist the boys help her convince the CO—whoever he is—that the rescue was actually a good thing.

No. That was the Kess I *knew*.

I have no idea what this girl is capable of.

VIVIENNE

THE CAPTAIN PACES the deck of the *Raptor*, cursing more colorfully than any of the dockworkers from my childhood, but by the time the royal barge pulls alongside and the liveried palace guard steps on deck, he is all brittle, leashed courtesy.

"Hello, sir." The captain tips his chin. "To what do I owe the honor?"

"We have come to collect what is rightfully ours." The guard nods at me.

"Surely you must know who and what she is," the captain says. "The admiralty will of course see that she returns to the palace after the trial."

"The minister for counterterrorism *does* know who and what she is," the guard replies coldly. "You may assure the admiralty that she will be made available when it is time for her to testify. Those noble lords are welcome to make arrangements to speak with her at the palace for any discussions or preparations that may be required."

The captain frowns. "The minister for counterterrorism? What does Ingannaro have to do with anything?"

"Ah. Of course you will not have heard, being at sea, but he is acting regent while the king's brothers return from the front."

It's all I can do to keep my face still. The minister for counterterrorism was a fleet admiral in the early days of the war and publicly decorated for valor in combat no fewer than six times. He holds a vast estate second only to the royal demesne. His brother is the minister for maritime infrastructure, and their great-grandfather was a baseborn son of the royal line.

I might be too late.

"Is that so?" Even though the captain's words are polite, there's an edge to them down deep. "It's been—how long— since the *Burying Ground* was expected to return to the neutral port after the signing? I know it can take time to get a message to the front, but this is taking a *long* time, yes?"

The palace guard turns to me and twitches his fingers like you might to call a dog. "Come here, child. The barge is waiting."

There's not a moment to lose. The minister for counterterrorism will be a formidable challenger, so the Royal Mother will need all the help she can get. Unless she has the seal, she doesn't have a chance.

"Don't worry, honey," the captain says to me. "Your part in this will be very easy. You've been through enough already. All you'll need to do is tell the judge that you were aboard the *Burying Ground* when it went down, and that the Duran girl was there, too."

I nod, slowly, because all that is true.

"You understand?" He smiles unexpectedly, as if he thought that would be harder. "Splendid. This will all be over soon."

"My lord?" I shuffle. "I . . . I must say more, yes? I must say how she did it?"

"Let us handle that part, all right?"

The palace guard nudges me and jerks his chin at the rope ladder, so I climb down and settle myself onto a seat. The guard joins us in the barge and gives a command to the oarsmen. They push away from the *Raptor* and we are off, carried by their strong, graceful strokes.

I fidget with the seal beneath my cuff. I ready myself.

I have been in the presence of the Royal Mother any number of times. She and my mistress shared an interest in art, so on their visits they would sit quietly by a window and draw or paint while I mended dresses on my stool in the corner and enjoyed the rare setting in which the princess seemed completely at ease.

I am not sure how I will be received now. *If* I will be received, when I survived and her own children did not. The Royal Mother does not strike me as that sort of person, but grief is as strange as the sea, and none of us move through it unchanged.

She will surely grant me an audience, even if it's just long enough to hand over the royal seal. The princess wouldn't do all the work of getting me here not to intervene one last time.

There is a small private dock, heavily guarded, reserved for official palace comings and goings. Once the royal barge is tied up, I step out of the swaying craft, and I am back on Ariminthian soil.

I expect that same rush of warmth and joy that I felt on the *Raptor*, seeing my homeland from afar, but all I feel is weariness.

I fall into step at the palace guard's elbow, and he whirls on me with an offended, incredulous look. I flinch and stumble back several paces, horrified.

All those days on my own. All those days with Cora in the jungle.

On the island I was someone else. Someone who did not think to walk three paces behind anyone of rank.

Someone untethered, a girl with no debts.

We are halfway up the dock when there's a faraway *boom*, and a tremor runs under me. I drop to a crouch out of habit, but there's no flying debris to avoid. After a moment, I straighten and turn in a slow circle, looking for the telltale gush of smoke. It rises in a haze from the west, thick and bulbous, and it won't be long till my nose stings from the chemicals and concrete dust.

One thing I have not missed is the explosions.

The palace guard grumbles something about the firing squad being too good for Duran saboteurs.

Soon the explosions and their carnage will be a distant memory. There will be peace. It won't be long now.

We enter the palace through one of the dozens of hidden doors, one I recognize as leading to the servants' quarters.

This is my duty. The sole reason the sea had mercy.

We walk down a long stone corridor and step into the chatelaine's sitting room. I remember it from that first day I was brought here, when she shoved me into that cupboard like a set of mismatched sheets.

The chatelaine rises from a blue cushioned armchair. She looks exactly the same as she did when I first arrived—a face like a flatiron and ageless like a witch.

Someone who could let a child cry till they were sick and remain unmoved.

She regards me like I'm a bucket of soiled diapers. "Don't think I've forgotten."

I am still. I don't even breathe.

"It was never my place to countermand her ladyship's choice," the chatelaine goes on. "Her fathers should have done that. There were plenty of suitable options for a lady's maid among the gentry."

None of them would take the job. Not since that fateful party where the princess spent the evening gibbering under a table, clutching the end of the lace tablecloth like a toddler with a security blanket while her helpless maid attempted to cajole her out.

"Well. That's in the past." The chatelaine dusts her hands like my life is crumbs. "You'll report to the underscullery. They'll find you work at the sinks."

Two basements beneath this floor, where the sun cannot reach and everything stinks of the whale oil lamps burning steadily, day and night.

The chatelaine is already turning back to her chair and the delicate teacup waiting for her when I say, "Yes. Only. First I must see the Royal Mother."

I'm trembling, every part of me, as she turns back, slow and incredulous.

"Excuse me?" Her voice is quiet, cut through with menace, reminding me that there are worse places than the under-scullery, that she is giving me a gift I don't deserve.

The royal seal bites into my wrist. I know I should show it to the chatelaine, but she will take it from me in an instant, slicing the cord from my wrist with her sewing scissors and rushing to the Royal Mother's side to present it herself.

That cannot be what the princess wants. She would not ask something like that of me.

So I stammer, "I—I would give the Royal Mother my condolences. The princess was my mistress. I would like to spend a few moments with someone else who loved her."

"I don't know who you think you are," the chatelaine goes on in that quiet razor of a voice, "but you are going to have some hard lessons coming if you think your ill-gotten time in royal company grants you any privileges."

"Besides, the Royal Mother is not in the palace at the moment," the guard informs me stiffly.

That can't be right. The Royal Mother would have come here as soon as it was clear the *Burying Ground* was late to return to the neutral port, so she would hear any news right away.

"She is keeping a private vigil at her villa," the guard goes on. "The minister for counterterrorism, as regent, has graciously agreed to ensure that she is not disturbed."

I nod calmly, as if I believe this is a good thing, but my stomach is writhing like it's full of salt water.

The minister for counterterrorism must know what I know about the king's brothers, that there is no direct heir to the throne. He must understand that the Royal Mother could become regent if enough of the noble lords see value in it, and he must believe that she has no plans to be his puppet.

Ingannaro will not be content to stay acting regent. The next thing he'll do is crown himself king and proclaim any challenger a traitor to Ariminthia. He'll do it quickly, too.

Dura is sure to go on the offensive, he'll say. *The realm must have a king to be secure.*

The chatelaine seizes my arm with a no-nonsense grip and steers me out of her sitting room, all but throwing me into the corridor.

"The underscullery," she repeats, cold and precise. "Unless you'd prefer the slaughterhouse or the charnel house."

I nod like my head is on a string. My feet are taking me along the corridor toward the narrow stone stairwell that leads down and down.

The Royal Mother is not even here. This was my one chance, and now it's gone for good.

The stairs are damp, the air stale. I go slow, plodding step on step on step. No reason to hurry now.

The other noble lords won't tolerate the minister for counterterrorism taking the throne. According to the sailors on the *Raptor*, those lords were gathering in the capital because they sensed something in the wind, and Ingannaro isn't the only one with a trace of royal blood.

There will be civil war. The Durans will hardly have to lift a finger. They'll produce a new treaty with whatever terms they like, just like the *Burying Ground* never happened.

You wouldn't want people to say she died for nothing.

I trail to a stop.

The sea is strange, but perhaps it can be wiser than us all. Had it not taken the princess, she would not have been able to help Cora, and had she not helped Cora, I would not have the royal seal.

The one thing that has any hope of preventing not only civil war, but the outright conquest of Ariminthia by a ruthless, brutal enemy.

She died for something. She died to save our homeland.

Only that won't happen if I stay here. It won't happen if I do what I'm told, the way I've done ever since my mother left me here.

On the island, I asked the princess to send me a sign, but the sea did not rise. The pirates did not find me.

Instead I walked the beaches untethered, and she sent a ship to save me.

The signs were always there. Always clear.

———

THE SERVANTS' ENTRANCE opens into a little warren of shacks and cottages that is usually thronging, and I'm surprised at how empty the streets are of housewives and dockworkers and children playing—until the caustic smell of creosote and smoldering concrete reminds me of the blast.

There will be roadblocks and checkpoints by now, manned by an elite counterterrorism constabulary who will detain and interrogate anyone who looks *shifty* or *resists arrest* or speaks the common language with an accent. Most people stay indoors after a bombing if they can, because Ingannaro's men take a certain pleasure in making everyone cower.

The city will remain locked down for at least a week unless the saboteurs are found, and I don't have a week to spare. Ingannaro's coup could happen at any time.

The Royal Mother's villa is not on the mainland. It's on a private island near the capital, and there's no proper dock— just a series of complicated elevators set into a sheer cliff. She does not like gendarmes and chose the location for her villa to eliminate the need for excessive security.

We always went by the royal barge, the princesses in their silk dresses on benches in the cabin, and the crown prince horsing around in the bow, pretending he was going to dive in or toss one of them overboard. The royal siblings would crowd, giggling, into the call box once we arrived and use ship-to-ship code to tap out a message on the pipes, and an operator would send the elevator down foot by creaking foot once she knew it was them.

I don't have a barge. I have no authority to use the call box.

Suddenly, irrationally, I wish Cora was here. She would come up with some half-baked plan that would seem ridiculous but get the job done, and she would act on it with the sort of unearned confidence that Durans seem to feel entitled to.

If Cora needed a boat, she'd just take one.

Well. I'm not Duran so I don't steal, but I could *borrow* a boat. And I know enough ship-to-ship code that I could plead my case with the call box operator.

A little wisp of energy goes through me, just *deciding* something like that.

But as I move toward the wharves, my stomach starts to sour. The burning smell grows stronger and more punishing, the smoke thicker and harsher. There are medic wagons on corners and nurses hurrying by with stretchers. People limp past, bloodied and dazed, and somewhere there's a baby crying.

The saboteurs must have hit the wharves. The area will be completely locked down and crawling with marines and gendarmes. The chances that I can borrow anything are nonexistent.

You have something to go back to.

I laugh aloud. I could try returning to the palace, but if I'm caught, the chatelaine will send me to the galleys—or the brothels—for insubordination.

Besides, the princess is counting on me. Ariminthia is counting on me.

The closer I get to the wharves, the more another smell whispers through the acrid reek of smoke and charred wood. The green, vibrant scent of brine that settled into the fibers of every room in that little house where I was happy, a girl with her nose pressed to the back window waiting for her papa to come home, while her mama sewed sea bags stitch on stitch.

After my mother left me at the palace, I never saw her again. Debtors have no days off, no holiday leave. If I had run away, even for an afternoon, not only would the constabulary have hauled me back, but my mother would have been sent to the galleys to make sure I had nowhere to go.

That little house might still be there, with its battered planter box out front full of pansies and basil. That big window that my mama said gave the best light in the house.

My feet remember the way. Past the pawnshop and downhill toward the harbor. There are hardly any people out, and

I keep expecting roadblocks, but the blast zone seems to be farther south, closer to Tideland Dock and the admiralty.

The house is just as I remember it, limewashed white with faded blue shutters. It's crowded together with two other houses like it, little dockworker shacks thrown up near the waterside for men who were all but part of the sea and women who sent their men to sail it and little girls who went to sleep lulled by its whispers.

The tide came right up under that house, set on pilings like it was, and my father kept a rowboat there. We'd go out in it on a fine day, and it always made me giggle to climb through the hatch in the kitchen floor, down the ladder, and into the boat without getting so much as my toes wet.

If that boat is still there, it will be less like stealing or even borrowing.

It will be like spending a few moments with my father one more time.

I should go around to the back of the house and see if that boat is still there. But I can't take my eyes off the front window, where my mama spent so many hours in that straight-backed wooden chair, murmuring her prayers and punching her needle through canvas.

She might still live here.

I'm moving across the street. I don't even know what I'll say if she opens the door. I haven't wept for her in years. She might be furious that I'm on her doorstep. She might be long gone. She—

It's not my mother who responds to my knock.

It's a man in a worn sea jacket, his skin lined from years of facing into salt winds. He takes one look at me and his mouth hangs open.

I can't breathe for more moments than I can count.

At last I whisper, "Papa?"

CORA

STAY CALM. TAKE your bearings.

Everything that kept me alive on the island, everything that gave me hope and confidence, everything that kept me safe from pirates—all in service of the kind of sabotage that Ariminthians constantly accuse us of, and we always deny.

All of it feels tainted now. Like if I use any of it to survive, I'm helping a government that's ready to let me die. I'm agreeing that sometimes it's okay to blow people up. Regular people. Even if they are Ariminthian.

And they're calling *me* a war criminal.

Use what the land gives you.

The room is empty but for the cot and blankets. The windows are nailed shut, and there are security bars on the outside. There are three terrorists in the kitchen making sure I don't try to leave.

I did not think things could get worse than the brig of the *Raptor*.

Down the hall, there's a faint clatter in the kitchen that I only belatedly realize is someone knocking on the door in that complicated pattern. Then there's a rumble of voices and footfalls.

No trees to climb. No jungle to hide in. I don't even have Alivarda's jackknife, as if I had any clue how to use it in anger.

I am out of options.

"Hey." There's a tap on the door and Kess leans in. Her voice is bright and her smile is too big. "Good news. We're moving you to a more secure location."

"You can shut up with that crap. I heard everything."

She sighs. "Don't make this harder than it needs to be."

"Kess." I fight down the choke in my voice. "Please. You have to help me."

"I tried. Believe me."

"What even *is* a CO?" I'm stalling.

"Commander of operations. My boss." Her voice takes an edge. "Seriously. You need to come now."

My mind is racing as I follow Kess down the dim hallway and into the kitchen. Rook and King are gone. The man waiting there is wearing a nondescript tunic and trousers, but it's clear he's nothing but muscle underneath. His graying dark hair and beard are cropped close, and his face doesn't seem the kind that smiles often.

On the counter behind him is a sandwich on a plate. The

filling oozes out the sides and the bread is stacked crooked, but it's food so I grab it with both hands and wolf a bite. It's some kind of flaky fish spread in a cream sauce and a slab of white cheese that might be on the brink of moldy, but I chew and chew like I've never seen food before.

"I know I'm in deep shit," Kess says to the CO, "but turning her over isn't right and you know it."

"Out of my hands, kiddo." The CO has a rumbly voice, deep, like a well with no bottom. "Command wants to see you, but we should debrief first. I'll meet you at the usual place. Off you go."

Kess nods. All at once she looks like she needs a year of sleep. She heads for the door, but on her way past, she leans close enough to mutter, "I'm sorry. I mean that. They say drowning's the most peaceful way to go. I hope that's true."

Then she's gone, leaving a flutter of dust as she pulls the door closed behind her.

I steady myself and face the CO. I'm trembling. "If you hand me over to the Ariminthians, that's the end of the cease-fire. We're back at war. That can't be what Parliament wants."

"It can, actually," the CO replies. "But it's not what the anti-war league wants. That's why I'm here to help you."

"The antiwar—you mean Embrace Piss?" I think of the letter pushed through our mail slot, the one with the unredacted report of what happened to my brother. The letter that was supposed to turn our family against the war once we knew what was *really happening*, according to their propaganda.

The CO makes a little half bow. "At your service. More properly the International Antiwar Coalition, but you can call it whatever you like as long as you hear me out."

"But Kess said you were her boss," I reply, "and she's a freaking *terrorist*. Embrace Piss is like five people who don't shower and wave homemade signs."

"Knight is an operative for the Duran government," the CO corrects. "She has nothing to do with the antiwar movement, and if she heard you suggest otherwise, she'd probably punch you. As for *Embrace Piss*, well, you only saw what the newspapers wanted you to see."

I ignore the cheap shot at my dad, even as his words go through my head. *The whole point is convincing people to see things your way, or reminding them how smart they are if they already agree with you.*

"The league has spent *years* orchestrating this treaty," the CO continues. "We are not prepared to stand by and watch everything we worked for fall apart."

"I don't understand. *What* work?"

"You didn't think the cease-fire happened because Crown and Parliament actually came to their senses, did you?"

No. I thought the cease-fire happened because Ariminthia was finally beaten down enough to hand over their extensive collection of maps, as well as the secrets of springwood so we could build ships as good as theirs.

"Truth is," the CO goes on, "because of us, because of the antiwar league, it's become all but impossible for Crown *or*

Parliament to wage war. We control both the shipping lanes and the high seas. We decide whether a cargo of Duran grain is going to reach its intended port or if an Ariminthian dreadnought can survive long enough to hassle one of those extraction colonies the industrialists love so much."

"Wait. Wait." I grip my sandwich. "It's the pirates who do that stuff. It's the *pirates* who raid Duran ships and make it so there's shortages and rationing."

"It's the one thing Crown and Parliament agree on—what to call the people who are forcing them to the peace table. Ariminthians and Durans, working together." He lifts his brows. "It's a hell of a lot more frightening than Embrace Piss."

My mouth is dry. "Pirates massacre people. My dad wrote about it all the time. They do terrible things to girls like me. They loot ships and—they were going to murder me and Vivienne on the island! We *heard* them!"

"Hold on." The CO peers at me. "One of our crews found you? My intel said you were arriving on an Ariminthian ship, but that didn't make sense. Ever since the *Burying Ground* sailed, the bulk of the Ariminthian navy has been here, on high alert, bracing for Duran forces to break the cease-fire. Direct orders from the counterterrorism minister."

"The pirates stole all our food," I snap. "Then they tried to hunt us down. They were prowling through the jungle all, *Come out, honey, we're not going to hurt you.* Like we're stupid or something."

The CO folds his arms. "Did anyone on that crew threaten you? *Ever?* Or did they tell you they'd come to help?"

They did. There on the sand after I ruined the shrine. They said not to be afraid, only we ran like hell because they were *pirates* and everyone knows what pirates do.

But what they did was investigate my signal fires. They kept searching the jungle even while their holds stayed empty, and they only left when the *Raptor* showed up.

"I saw two pirates with a sea chest full of gold and silver coins," I retort. "They tried to bury it without anyone knowing. How does *that* help along peace?"

"Peace isn't free. We need food and supplies. Ships. We send wages home to our families. What, you think we can just walk into a bank and make a deposit?"

Gold and silver coins. Ariminthian thalers and Duran florins.

You only saw what the newspapers wanted you to see. I sure as hell didn't want to see a secret Duran military training program for children.

"So you're saying that the pirates aren't really pirates," I reply. "They belong to Embrace Piss?"

"There are real pirates, that much is true. Vicious sons of guns, out for their own gain, and then there's us. The antiwar league. What I'm saying is that those who govern call antiwar volunteers *pirates* so the likes of you and I will blame them for everything bad that the war brings." The CO's voice sharpens. "*All* who govern. Crown and Parliament alike."

"But you're pretty sure the pirates who were on the island with me and Viv were there to help us."

"We're the only ones actively looking for survivors," he says. "Not the Crown. Not Parliament. Us. Embrace Piss."

I snort. "How do *you* know?"

"Kiddo, I run five covert ops teams. I know what every member of the Ariminthian cabinet had for breakfast this morning. And don't get me started on those clowns in Parliament."

There were never going to be any medals. No ceremonies, no dinner parties, no spotlight.

"Have you found anyone else?" I can't keep the tremble out of my voice because I want to know, but also I don't. "Other survivors?"

The CO shakes his head, but he must see something in my face because he adds, "But that doesn't mean we've stopped looking. Or that they're not out there."

I'm still holding my half-eaten sandwich. This fish paste is pretty awful, but I finish the last few bites and try not to think how the one may be true, but the other just might not.

"So you decided to go against Parliament to help me," I say, and I know I should be upset by that, but instead a small wisp of hope warms my belly for the first time since that meeting with the captain of the *Raptor*. "Does that mean you're going to help me get home?"

"Uhhh." The CO rubs the back of his neck ruefully. "About that."

PIRATES

VIVIENNE

IT'S HIM. MY father. He's all angles now, and weather-beaten like the buoy we both once swam to, me in my little red bathing suit before the gendarmes marched him out of sight.

"Lambkin," he whispers, and the years fall away and I am small and there's a chair pushed against the kitchen window and I am watching for him, waiting for him to come up the beach in his heavy dockworker boots and greatcoat.

"They'd have sent you to the tidal cages." My voice isn't much above a whisper, and it's raspy like sandpaper. "How are you here?"

"Inside. Quickly." My father holds the door open wider and I duck through, under his arm and into that sitting room, my hopes jumbled and teeming.

The chair is still under the window, but it's empty.

The whole house is empty when once there was a rag rug

and a shelf with a little plant and rows of washed-up sea glass we found. The room is chilly, too, no fire in the grate, and it's clear that my father doesn't live here.

No one lives here anymore.

He opens his arms for a hug, and I know I'm meant to run to him. I'm meant to throw myself against him and breathe deeply the smell of him.

I stay where I am.

My father's smile falters, and he lets his arms drop to his sides. He says nothing, only looks at me. Like if he just looks hard enough, or long enough, he can see me at twelve, or thirteen, or any of those years he missed. I keep waiting for him to speak, to say how sorry he is, to beg my forgiveness.

I am remembering how hard I cried when he was taken away, how my mother shushed me in front of the gendarmes in case they mistook us all for traitors. I am remembering how it felt like my very world was ending and I could do nothing about it but cry.

"She sold me to the palace, you know," I say into the silence. "Remunerative servitude. She had to. Did you know that?"

My father nods. "It broke my heart."

"But that didn't stop you, did it? You knew what would happen to Mama, to me, if you kept going to those meetings. You knew what would happen to *you*." I laugh bitterly. "Only you escaped somehow, and Mama and I didn't."

My father runs both hands through his hair. He does not reply, but his eyes grow shiny.

"Then *why*?" I choke on it. "You didn't have to *like* the war. You could have just kept quiet about it. Plenty of people do—even people in the palace! Why couldn't you have just . . ."

"Done nothing?" My father smiles crookedly.

My heart is growing heavier by the moment. I should have simply gone for that blasted rowboat.

"Lambkin, I did nothing for as long as I could. I went to the docks and unloaded cargo. I boarded those sloops and dreadnoughts when commanded. I sewed up friends in their hammocks and gave them to the sea. I came home and watched your mama stitch those bags endlessly for more and more boys. For years I did those things. Years before you were born. Then years after. You know what I never saw?"

I shake my head.

"One of our noble lords given to the sea," he says. "They love the war, every man of them, but they don't love fighting, or *dying*, so they leave that part to us."

Little wonder my mother called his friends traitors and blasphemers, if this is the kind of thing he can just *say*.

It's the kind of thing Cora would say. She *did* say it.

There's basically no reason for them if they're not always thinking about war, or planning for war, or sending their bailiffs around to extract taxes to pay for the war.

The Ariminthian nobility will fight to the last peasant before they'll admit defeat.

I was born here, in this little house by the wharf, and in my early years, I thought I knew what would become of me. There was comfort in knowing I'd grow up and sew sea bags for sailors and marines just like my mama.

Then my father was arrested for being a member of the antiwar league.

Then I went into remunerative servitude.

And then—one morning the chatelaine was ill, and her assistant sent me abovestairs to collect fireplace grates for blackening. All the chambers should have been empty, but in a room with flocked wallpaper and mahogany wainscoting, a princess of the royal line huddled beneath her vanity table trying to be overlooked so she would not have to attend a state dinner.

You could just be ill, I said, both hands full of filthy iron grates smudging my sackcloth dress and flaking soot onto the mohair carpet. *Not every time. Not twice in a row. But sometimes.*

I was not born to be a lady's maid—and the closest thing Princess Aubrielle Melisande Felicity Tiralie Vivienne of Ariminthia ever had to a friend—but it happened.

"The antiwar league saved you from the tidal cages," I say to my father here, now, in the shadowy dim of the sitting room in the house where I grew up.

"The Crown doesn't want anyone to know that some of

those it has condemned as traitors are still alive, that we have been successful at anything, so officially we died horribly in the cages. The league has many ghosts." He squints at me. "But how can you be here? You belong to the palace."

"I . . . I have borrowed myself," I admit, because even though I do not steal, I'm not sure how I will return myself once I have fulfilled my task. Or if I will return myself.

"Borrowed yourself." My father laughs approvingly, and the sound fills every corner of this little house just as it did when I was small.

A soft scrape of wood on wood whispers from the bedroom.

"That'll be my colleague." My father steps inside the small empty space. "He's bringing a girl for me to hide. Once she arrives, I must take her somewhere safe right away. I'm too well known on the docks to stay here long."

I am a girl you could have hidden.

I can't find a way to say it, though. My palace voice is all wrong, and I don't know if I have another.

I get to the bedroom doorway in time to see a small hatch in the wall swing open on hinges that were not there when I was a child.

Or maybe it's that I did not know about that hatch or those hinges. Maybe my father did his best to ensure our safety by keeping his own secrets.

A man crouches through, stooping low and cursing in the

common language. A push of cold wharfside air comes in with him, briny and fresh, and he holds the little door open for someone behind him.

The girl my father is meant to hide comes through crouching, same as the man, but I recognize her right away. Cora glances around the room with that practiced sweep I remember from the jungle, the one she must have been trained to do to survey a space for threats.

The antiwar league has rescued her, same as they did for my father.

We lock eyes, and I brace for her anger. Even though there was nothing I could do for her on the *Raptor*. Even though my father is about to help her.

But she grins. She grins and whispers, "Viv! Are you in the *antiwar league?*"

I begin to tell her of course not, that those sentiments are a one-way trip to the tidal cages and blasphemy besides.

But those people saved my father. Because of them, he is alive to help her and he is alive to be standing in the house where I grew up.

My father and the man who brought Cora exchange a brisk handshake. They confer briefly, then the man slips back out the hatch.

Perhaps he is also a ghost.

"It seems you're to be a guest of the league," my father says to Cora. "Wait here. I will call you when it's time to go."

He moves past us both and into the kitchen, but Cora ignores his instructions and follows. I trail after, keeping to the doorway.

Keeping my distance.

There's an old hurricane lamp on the counter, and my father sparks it to life. He produces a flat silver square from his pocket about the size of his palm. It opens like a clamshell, and inside is a disk of red glass. He uses the glass and lamplight to flash a staggered pattern out the window, toward the inky harbor.

"What is he doing?" Cora is at my elbow. She seems more subdued now. Numb, almost.

I am remembering how my father would stand with a lamp at the kitchen window long after supper, his back to the room as if studying the waves. In less than a turn of the glass, he would kiss my mama and me, then whisk himself out of the house with a story about a card game or an odd job.

"My father is signaling to his friends in the antiwar league," I reply, because that is what he was doing then as well, and I was just too small or too foolish to realize it.

"Your—that's your *dad*?"

Cora sounds at once wondering and envious, and I remember what she spat at me while in the brig of the *Raptor*.

You have something to go back to. I'm a freaking orphan now.

My breath leaves me all at once. The princess did not see fit to simply save Ariminthia by setting all this in motion. She also means to offer me something she believes is a reward.

She has given me something—some*one*—to go back to.

Princess Aubrielle Melisande Felicity Tiralie Vivienne of Ariminthia would have me forgive my father.

THE WORST PART isn't what Command's going to do. I could take being drummed out or dumped in the deepest hole in the stockade or busted down to desk work. I could even take being put against the wall if it comes to that.

I can't take that chess team is never going to trust me again.

I still don't see what else I could have done. Someone put that intel in the dead drop. Someone with red envelope clearance.

Duran survivor of the Burying Ground *to be transported by wagon to Tideland Dock. Charge is war crimes. No extraction authorized.*

I asked, *Now what?* I got an answer.

The worst part is that chess team didn't see it. They didn't see what a complete disaster shitshow it would have been to let that prison wagon continue on its merry way, to let the Ariminthians decide what happened to the *Burying Ground*.

As soon as chess team learned the rescue wasn't a direct order, they no longer had my back. They didn't see how I did the right thing, even if that meant going against Command.

Against Parliament, even.

The *usual place* is a shed behind a sad little brothel in the shanty district. I sit on an upturned bucket and keep an exit handy. In a while there's a sentry tap, and the CO slides inside.

"They're going to be using words like *insubordination*," he says. "What's your story going to be?"

I've been thinking about this. "Rook and King had no idea. I convinced them there were orders to rescue Cora, and I stand behind pulling her out. Besides, how can I be insubordinate? Chess team hasn't received a direct order since we were told to keep tabs on pirate movement."

"You engaged in a combat action during the cease-fire." He says it mildly, not like an accusation. "All of covert ops received that cease-fire order months ago."

"It was a *rescue* action," I reply. "One that Command should have authorized and planned, so it could have been done with a hell of a lot more finesse than I could manage on short notice."

The CO raises an eyebrow, and I know he's right. Saying stuff like that is only going to make things worse.

"Okay, fine. I did skirt that nonviolence directive, and I did use more gelignite in my distraction than was strictly necessary because, okay, *yes*, my fingers were itchy and surveillance is coma-inducingly boring." I cut a glance at him. "But Chief, you *know* me. I follow orders, even ones that make no sense. Even ones I don't like. Even ones that *reek* of frigging politics. But this was different. *No* extraction? Not even to find out what she knows? Not even to shout her innocence into the counterterrorism minister's smug face whether it's true or not?"

The CO doesn't reply, only folds his arms, and I can't tell him what I really think. I'm in enough trouble as it is.

"Doing nothing didn't sit right, okay?" I mutter it, because this is me basically admitting to insubordination. "Sure, this is war. But even in war there's right and wrong, and this . . ."

I shrug uncomfortably. I don't know how to finish, but the CO waits. The silence grows heavy and awkward.

"So I guess that's my story." I square up. "It wasn't right. So I did something about it."

"Some might call that treason."

My hands go in fists, and I start to tell him off because I *will not* be lumped in with those shitbirds in Embrace Piss. They're the ones who won't just shut their pieholes and let us win the war. They're the ones who can't just read the papers instead of making up the wildest nonsense about Parliament and the industrialists.

But then I shut up. I shut up and slump on the bucket because *traitor* rolls off the tongue real easy when you don't like what someone's doing because it makes you look bad.

"Command is going to want to know how you knew about the prison wagon," the CO says into the quiet. "That information was being held very close to a lot of vests."

Whoever put that intel in the dead drop must feel the same way I do, and they must not be in a position to act. They probably took a massive risk just to tip their hand, and I have no intention of hanging them out to dry.

"Dock chatter," I tell him.

The CO's face doesn't change, and I am only now realizing that whoever provided that intel has red envelope clearance and knows I'm the one who checks chess team's dead drop.

They knew I was the one who asked, *Now what?*

"I guess the captain of that ship Cora was on sent messages by carrier bird to the admiralty." I shrug. "Their security sucks."

The CO nods slowly. Command has gotten intel this way before, so it's plausible I could have as well. We rely on wharf-side convos for a reason.

"Right. Well." He rubs his beard. "It'll be all but impossible to prove otherwise if that's your story."

"That's my story."

"Hmm." The CO peers at me. "You might survive this after all, kiddo, but things are going to go hard for you. At the very least, you'll be reassigned."

Chess team is done for good because of me. No wonder Rook and King left the way they did, without a word, in two different directions.

"I know," I reply.

"Probably sent home."

"I know."

"Was it worth it?"

It's unexpected, which is likely why I don't hesitate. "Yes. Absolutely. And I'd do it again."

The CO cocks his head. "Interesting."

CORA

VIVIENNE'S DAD TURNS from the window. "This is taking too long. Something's wrong."

I barely hear him. I'm still reeling.

You can't go back to Dura. Not until the treaty's signed. Maybe not even then.

"I'll have to fetch a boat myself." He presses something small and cold into my hand. "If you see any pattern of blinking lights from the harbor, use this to send a response. Two short flashes. Keep it with you, wherever they take you. Understand?"

Sure. Flash some pirates. Whatever.

I slip the metal square into my pocket. It lands with a gentle thud where Alivarda's knife used to be.

If you come home, if you publicly exist as a survivor of the Burying Ground, *one party will gain the upper hand at the other's expense. One smells like roses; the other looks like monsters. But if the Ariminthians execute you publicly and hideously, both parties* can roundly condemn it. Both can agree that a renewed offensive is not only appropriate, but justified.

Both can win.

There's some padding footfalls and then the faint squeal of hinges. Vivienne is murmuring in Ariminthian. Her voice is low and fervent, something like wonder. She is still staring out the window at the black shimmers in the harbor.

The counterterrorism minister is firmly running the show here while they figure out who'll be king next. He absolutely intends to see you in those cages, whatever it takes.

"Cora?" Vivienne sounds more cheerful than she has any right to be. "You were likely taught to steal in your invasion training. Can you steal a boat for me?"

I start to get angry before it occurs to me that she's right. *Use what the land gives you. Anything you find belongs to the enemy and is therefore fair game.*

"Maybe." I shrug listlessly, but something makes me glance at her. "Didn't your dad go to find a boat?"

"That doesn't matter. I will be gone from here by the time he returns."

That gets through. "Hold on. Your dad's supposed to find me a safe place to stay. You're coming with us, right?"

"I can't go with my father now. I have another task. One that can't wait."

"One that needs a boat." I'm rallying. "One you don't want your dad to know about."

Vivienne studies the harbor. Then she holds out her wrist,

shaking back the oversize cuff. There's a gold charm secured to it, and all at once I remember her tying it there when we had to swim to the warship and escape the pirates. The fabric scrap has dug an angry red line into her skin.

"This is the royal seal of Ariminthia," she says. "Whoever has it will be well positioned to be the next ruler. All of the old king's brothers are dead—may the ocean keep them—so I must get this seal to the Royal Mother. That means I need a boat. You know how to steal and you're good at it, so the princess has sent you here to see that I get one."

"I'm sorry—*what*?"

Vivienne starts talking, but I don't understand a word of it, even though she's using the common language. Something about the princess and the island and the sea teaming up to take care of us and bring us together, about the suitcase I found and the boat that used to be tied up under this house, and how everything that has happened since the loss of the *Burying Ground* has been for one reason only: so there would be peace, the way the princess wanted.

"I must get to the Royal Mother," Vivienne says. "If she becomes regent, she will seek peace. The minister for counter-terrorism will never agree to peace. Not unless Dura surrenders unconditionally. He does not like the idea of your people having any of our secrets that the treaty will grant. Not our maps, and certainly not springwood. He would have us *win* the war, and the noble lords who feel the same will back him. The ones who believe they should be king instead will fight him, and there will be civil war. The loss of the *Burying Ground* will be for nothing."

Her voice warps. We have this between us, at least.

"Right." I peer at her. "But how do you know that the Royal Mother would sign the treaty? How do you know she doesn't feel the same way?"

"My mistress would not have made all this happen if that were true." Vivienne is serene, utterly confident. "The Royal Mother will make peace if it's in her power."

"Okay. But I . . . don't see how your plan works." I say it as politely as I can. "We learned in school that the Royal Mother isn't royal at all. There's some kind of weird rule that says her children with the king are his heirs, but she doesn't have to be married to the king because he's married to someone else."

"It's not a *weird rule*," Vivienne replies sternly. "It's a holy rite. A sacred spiritual union. There's no need to be rude about it."

I shrug impatiently because I'm not trying to be rude. "What I mean is, why wasn't she on the *Burying Ground*?"

"According to the treaty terms, each side was to bring their families, yes? But just their closest family. Not aunts or uncles or grandparents. The Royal Mother is that way. Dearly loved but not closest. Not a member of the royal family."

I'm not sure what to make of that, but then again, plenty of kids from training had parents who split up and then married other people. I guess it's not *too* weird. Just a little hard-core, knowing your dad doesn't think of your mom as close family just because the two of them aren't together.

"She has no claim to a royal title," Vivienne adds, "but she could be named regent. Supporting the Royal Mother's authority in this way would allow the noble lords to save face in front of one another and back away from civil war, but only if there's a clear sign that she is meant to rule."

Vivienne holds out her wrist once more, and the seal turns a wink of gold light from the hurricane lamp.

"The sea means for you to be a part of this. I don't know why. Its ways are not for us to know. But you are here. You want peace, and so does she." Vivienne hesitates. "So do I."

The sea is just the sea. It can't want things. But there's no denying that it can *do* things, and even though I don't quite believe it could have intent, I honestly have no other way to account for any of this, from how I survived the wreck in the first place to how I came to be standing in Vivienne's childhood home with a very real chance to end this war.

My dad would call it coincidence. My mom would call it luck. But string together enough lucky breaks, enough coincidence, and they start to become ways that are not for us to know.

So maybe Vivienne is right. Maybe this is the sea's doing. Maybe her princess really meant for me to be here, right now, for a reason.

A red light winks from the harbor. Two blinks. Then three. I pull the silver mirror case out of my pocket.

Maybe it's time to hear what the sea has in mind.

VIVIENNE

CORA MUTTERS SOMETHING about how she would gladly never *look* at another boat as long as she lives, but she climbs through the hatch in the kitchen floor, down the rope ladder, and into the waiting rowboat like she was born doing it.

I don't invite her. She just comes. I know better than to question the sea and its ways.

By the time I join her in the boat, she is lecturing the captain of the small vessel on his lateness. If he's surprised to see two girls in cabin boy trousers, he doesn't say anything. When no one else comes down the ladder, he quietly bids the oarsmen to bring us clear.

The wharfside is sleeping, as much as it ever sleeps, when our boat glides out from under my house and into the bay. The night is deep and endless, the stars in full scatter. I'm perched on a bench next to one of the oarsmen. He's hooded against the sea spray like the rest of them, and aside from grunting acknowledgment when I sat down, he has not so much as glanced at me.

Perhaps it's safer this way. If we are caught, neither of us can betray the other.

My eyes adjust to the dark, and the heavy bulk of warships and sloops anchored in the harbor rise from the sea like great beasts. Lanterns glow at the masts and rails, and there are sure to be sailors on watch.

We move steadily, silently, through the edges of darkness, out of the reach of those soft fans of orange light.

"Right," Cora says into the stillness. "I don't know anything about these blinky mirror things, so I don't know what Viv's dad told you—flashed at you?—but we need to go to the Royal Mother's villa."

The captain scoffs. "The minister for counterterrorism has stationed half a dozen sloops around her private landing. I won't put my crew at risk like that. I'll take you somewhere safe, but I won't bring you there."

"Hi, hello, I'm the war criminal." Cora makes a little half wave from her bench in front of mine. "You've all taken a lot of chances to save me from being horribly executed, and I really appreciate that, but none of it's gonna matter if there's no peace treaty. Right? I can't tell you a lot right now, but I can tell you this: all your antiwar pirate work goes down the crap chute unless we get to that villa."

The captain lifts a brow. "You're awfully sure of yourself."

"Someone's got to be regent, right? It can be the counter-terrorism minister, or it can be the Royal Mother. Ingannaro sure as hell has no plans to sign a treaty. The way Vivienne tells it, he seems kind of *happy* that the *Burying Ground* went down. He is a *bad freaking choice*." Cora turns to me. "Right, Viv?"

I don't know what voice to use. My palace voice is not right, and I can't find the one I had before.

"He doesn't seem upset about the *Burying Ground*, no. Or surprised, for that matter." The captain squints at her. "When you come right down to it, he's the one who had plenty of chances to sabotage that ship. He made no secret of his thoughts on the treaty, and given how quick he was to seize power . . . it does suggest a motive."

"Viv?" Cora presses. "You have to know something. You spent all that time in the palace."

"Not really," I reply, but that is not exactly true. The minister for counterterrorism is the one who supervised the construction of the ship. He's the one who made a show of searching Cora three times simply because she was the right age for a saboteur.

He's the one who made himself regent before the shrines were so much as thought of, and even now he keeps the Royal Mother in her villa with some story about privacy.

The oarsmen have stopped rowing, and we are drifting in the black harbor. From here we can see the silent fleet of sloops scattered in front of the Royal Mother's landing. Some lie at anchor while others patrol in lazy patterns, their lanterns like stars pulled to earth.

This does not feel like protecting someone's privacy.

"The Royal Mother's regency would be tenuous," the captain says thoughtfully. "The noble lords would need convincing. She would need all the support she could muster."

"You could help her," Cora puts in. "The pirates, I mean. Hey, you totally *should*! You both want the same thing, and she could give all the pirates a pardon for the bad stuff they've been doing. And if it's true how you basically ground this whole war to a giant standstill, you must have a *lot* of force to bring to bear. A lot to need a pardon for, too."

The captain grunts in a noncommittal way, but my heart turns to mush. My father would no longer have to be a harbor ghost, but it would not give back the years we spent apart.

It would not give back the years he turned away from.

"Well, it may not matter." The captain pulls a spyglass from his greatcoat pocket and studies the blockade. "Those are fast ships. We can't run past them, and we can't fight so many."

"We could go around to the other side of the island, to the Bay of the Drowned Maidens." I gesture to a forbidding headland. "There's a lighthouse where emergency ladders are kept. In case something happens to the elevator."

The captain takes my measure. "Is it safe for my crew?"

"The sea takes no one before their time." I recite the

proverb before I remember that not all antiwar pirates are Ariminthian. I have no idea how the sea feels about Durans. So I add, "There are shoals, but the night is calm and the tide will be in."

The captain nods, squints at the Royal Mother's island for a long moment, then puts his hand up. One by one, the crew does the same, and it occurs to me that they are deciding together whether the risk is warranted.

I cannot help but admire the simplicity of it, the way each person can use their voice without saying a word, before it occurs to me that they are voting.

This is what voting can be like.

Every pirate puts his hand up, agreeing to row us there. There's a brief discussion about the safest way to proceed, then the sailors dig their oars into the water and move us silently in a wide arc around the patrol fleet.

I press the royal seal against my wrist till it stings. Otherwise I will start remembering my father when I really ought to be forgetting him once more.

Otherwise I will start reckoning how the Royal Mother has every right to send me back to the palace once this errand is complete, how my time of making choices will draw to a close.

The oarsman next to me has stopped rowing. His paddle hovers over the water, dripping bright gems, and he is staring openly at the royal seal at my wrist.

Perhaps he is wishing he'd stayed in bed instead of agreeing to ferry two traitors past a flotilla ready to sink any ship that comes near the Royal Mother.

"I'm sorry," I murmur in the common language, and as I pull my cuff over the seal, I glance at him sidelong—and gasp aloud.

He is the crown prince of Ariminthia.

"My lord!" It comes out a strangled whisper because I watched him die. I watched that spar come down and break his back, and I would have heard the noise he made had the roar of wind and surf not spared me that.

The oarsman scowls, and in that moment I realize he's not the crown prince. He's older and broader across the shoulders, and his cheekbones are sharper, but the resemblance is startling.

"You're thinking of someone else," he mutters.

I am remembering the crown prince, how he'd spur his horse through the marketplace without heed for goods or children. How he'd buy round after round at an alehouse, running up a tab that he'd leave to the landlord. How he spent his days in the palace war room instead of taking a fleet commission.

Cora swivels on the seat in front of me. "Hey. So. Am I translating this right? Are we really going to a place called the *Bay of the Drowned Maidens?*"

I nod, but my attention is on the oarsman who now is putting his back into his rowing and deliberately not looking at me.

"What is it with you Ariminthians and giving things such scary, ominous names? I would much rather be going to Happy Sunshine Bay right now and, really, a ship meant to carry a peace delegation should be called the *Fluffy Kitten* or something. What did you lot pick? The *Burying Ground*." Cora smiles, likely to show she's trying to make light of it. "My dad said the king probably chose the name to remind everyone what was at stake, that it would be peace or death."

"Not everyone," mutters the oarsman.

"Sorry, what was that?" Cora asks.

The oarsman who isn't the crown prince mumbles something in Ariminthian that he clearly doesn't want her to understand.

But I do.

"Ariminthians give their dead to the sea," I tell Cora. "The Durans are the ones who bury people in the soil."

"But that means—ohhhh." Cora frowns, then bristles a little. "It was a threat."

The oarsman doesn't break his steady rhythm.

"That's how you can know it wasn't the king who named that ship." I turn to the oarsman and ask, "That's what you said just now, yes?"

The oarsman looks up, and the moonlight planes his face into the likeness of the king on a gold thaler coin.

Missing. Presumed captured.

The palace mourned the king's youngest brother in secret for an entire year. The king and his consort built a magnificent shrine with their own hands in a private courtyard behind high walls and a door with three locks. They filled it with objects that belonged to him to call him to it and buried vast treasures beneath. We all thought the king's youngest brother satisfied and at home there, since he never once haunted the palace.

"Because you knew the king was willing to consider an honorable peace," I say to the oarsman in Ariminthian. "If you really were an antiwar pirate, my lord, you'd lump him in with the noble lords who prefer endless war to giving up a single map."

"You are mistaken," the oarsman replies mildly in the common language, "and if you don't leave off this *my lord* business, these lads will bust my—ah, will give me no end of teasing."

"Mistaken about what?" Cora asks.

"Your friend thinks I'm someone I'm not. Someone who died years ago."

Your friend. It stills me, there in that rowboat gliding soundlessly across the harbor. But Cora doesn't turn a hair.

"Can't be the king. I mean, you look a lot like the picture of him from my history book, but he only died recently." Cora considers. "Can't be one of his brothers, either. They're all dead as well, and that's why we're taking the seal to the Royal Mother."

"Two are dead," I reply quietly. "The other one vanished. Missing, presumed captured. None of this is public knowledge, though. The palace made very sure of that."

The oarsman closes his eyes. "He's dead. I assure you. And even if he isn't, he will not return."

I have no memory of the king's brothers. They were young men all, no wives or heirs, and they became naval commanders long before I entered service at the palace.

But I've never been more sure of anything.

"How can you just . . . *not return*?" It comes out wild, nowhere near my palace voice, because it does not seem possible. Not for someone like the king's youngest brother.

Not for someone like me.

Cora is frowning, confused. "I thought if you lived in a monarchy, you didn't get to make your own choices. You have to do what you're told."

"Is it so different where you're from? Or just dressed up better?" The oarsman smiles at her. "Pirates make all their own choices. They may be foolish choices, and you might not get to make them for long, but they are *yours*."

My father did nothing for as long as he could. Or rather, he did as he was told, but then he started making his own choices.

He did not even have the princess to help him, or the island to guide his steps or hands or heart or mind.

"The king was sure that the Durans captured you, but it was the antiwar pirates, wasn't it?" I ask the oarsman quietly. "You learned the truth about them, but more than that, for the first time you could do whatever you wanted. Not what your parents or your brothers or anyone said you could do. Or had to do. You could do what you thought was right."

The oarsman doesn't reply. He merely digs the long paddle into the water, drags it back with one steady motion, then does it again.

"No wonder you died," Cora says cheerfully into the silence.

When he cracks a smile, he looks so much like the crown prince that it takes my breath away.

But I am remembering how the king's youngest brother went missing, how everyone figured they knew what had happened to him because there was no other possibility.

I am thinking how something very similar happened to my father.

I am wondering how something like that could happen to me.

CORA

I DON'T KNOW a lot about the sea, or landmarks, or anything like that, but the Bay of the Drowned Maidens sure doesn't look like a bay.

It looks like a sheer freaking cliff.

One that Vivienne honestly thinks we're going to climb with a ladder made of rope. No safety harness. No net. Nothing between us and the churning water and whatever rocks are hiding beneath.

I'm starting to get an idea how those maidens may have drowned in the first place.

There's a lighthouse at the top, clinging to the edge, and if I crane my neck, I can spot the beacon. The pirates nudge the boat into a shallow half-moon in the rocks, and one of them produces a little mirror like the one Vivienne's dad gave me, only this one is a regular mirror and not red glass. The pirate angles the mirror so it catches the beacon light in a series of flashes.

"Are they in the antiwar league as well?" I ask, bewildered, but the captain shakes his head.

"Nah. Just a standard hail, and an appeal in ship-to-ship code."

After what feels like an eternity, there are answering winks from the top of the cliff. Then there's a muffled thudding sound of something slithering down the rock face. The pirates dig their paddles into the choppy water and maneuver us toward it. We're all but bumping the cliff when I can make out the thick damp ropes lashed together into a ladder, black with tar.

"It will be better if I go first," Vivienne says. "The lighthouse keepers will know me. They will not cut the ropes and send me into the sea."

I shiver, and not just from the spray.

The boat sways as Vivienne rises, and soon she is moving carefully up the side of the cliff face hand over hand.

"The good part about going second is that you can benefit from any of her mistakes," the captain tells me, but I must look horrified because he adds, more kindly, "Don't worry. Half my crew is Duran, and they'll tell you that they float same as anyone else."

"Sorry." I laugh a little to make him feel better. "Being this close to water again is kind of freaking me out. Especially in the Bay of the Drowned Maidens when I've nearly been one myself—twice."

The captain pats the side of the rowboat. "I understand. You probably had more than your fill of little boats like this after the *Burying Ground*. How long were you adrift?"

"Adrift?" I frown. "You mean, in a lifeboat? Nope. Those fell apart with the rest of the ship."

"Fell apart," the captain repeats, like he's trying and failing to translate. Like he's too tactful to ask whether I mean *blown apart*.

"I don't care what anyone tells you." I say it clear and precise. "There was no blast. There was a storm, and less than a minute after the rain started coming down in sheets, the whole deck broke into pieces like a spilled box of matchsticks. The sails collapsed, and the ropes and everything, and that brought down the masts. The rest of the ship sort of . . . dissolved."

"May the ocean keep them." The captain makes a little waving motion with one finger over his heart.

"Some people did manage to launch the lifeboats," I add quietly, "but those turned into mushy sawdust within minutes of touching the water. Like everything else. There was nothing to grab on to. Nothing to help keep you afloat."

The captain waits politely while I scrub and scrub at my eyes.

"If the sea intends to take a ship, it usually begins with the hull." He taps his boot against the bottom of the rowboat. "The deck of a warship is difficult to breach. It would take some doing to make it fall apart the way you describe."

He doesn't say it mean, like he's calling me a liar, but more like he's thinking it through. Wondering how it might have happened.

"Cap." One of the sailors gestures with a thumb to the top of the cliff face, where there are two quick winks of a mirror, then two more.

Time to get this over with.

I tug a few times on the ladder. It seems like it'll still hold my weight, so the lighthouse keeper must have recognized Vivienne.

The captain puts a staying hand on my arm. "You're not wrong. The antiwar movement has a lot of resources at its disposal, and we could give the Royal Mother the show of force she'd need to make her regency viable. That decision isn't mine to make, though. I can present it to leadership, but that will take time."

"I don't know that we have time," I reply. "It sounds like the counterterrorism minister is polishing the crown as we speak."

"There's also the question of whether the Royal Mother will accept our help," the captain says. "The palace has put hundreds of my friends in the tidal cages for lèse majesté over the years. Taking help from so-called traitors—she risks looking like a traitor herself."

My heart plummets, because of course the Royal Mother won't take their help. She might not be a part of the royal family, but she is Ariminthian, and she is not going to compromise.

But Vivienne did. She and I survived the jungle and rescued ourselves through a million tiny compromises.

"Here's my proposal," the captain says. "I'll go to leadership with this . . . opportunity. You will determine whether the Royal Mother will accept our help. She must understand that the price is unconditional amnesty for anyone who has ever had anything to do with the antiwar movement, including a full pardon for acts they took in its name."

I nod slowly, not because I think I can do that on my own, but because I hope Vivienne can.

"If leadership agrees to back the Royal Mother, my crew and I will return to this bay at the next full moon. We will wait till dawn. If she wants our help and agrees to our terms, signal me with five flashes." The captain gestures to my pocket. "Use the red mirror, not an ordinary one."

"We'll see what happens," I say, and I turn once more toward the ladder. The rowboat lurches and my feet skid in the sludge at the bottom.

The deck of a warship is difficult to breach. If the sea intends to take a ship, it usually begins with the hull.

"Captain?" I say over my shoulder. "What sorts of things *could* ruin a deck?"

He squints. "A shoddy build would do it. Cheap labor. Poor-quality materials. Rushed out of the shipyard. Ariminthians don't build shoddy, though. We don't dare. The sea takes enough of us as it is. And the *Burying Ground* was built to impress."

The sludge at the bottom of the boat catches moonlight and gleams. Like oil.

"What if you spilled something on it?" I ask.

"Springwood's pretty durable," the captain replies skeptically. "You'd have to get whatever it was down in the meat of the wood somehow."

The mirror flashes again at the same time the ladder dances

impatiently against the cliff face, so I thank each of the pirates, take a deep breath, and grab good firm handholds.

I look up and up.

"Stay calm," I whisper, because it's good advice, and I want the voice in my head to be my own.

———

THE WIND SLAMS the ladder and me both against the cliff face, and my fingers slide along the tarry rungs like they're greased. The sea spray is blinding.

It's nothing like going up a tree. Nowhere near.

By the time I approach the top, my arms are throbbing and Alivarda's clothing hangs off me like a sodden shroud.

As I'm trying to figure out how to get myself up and over the cliff edge, a pair of sturdy hands grabs me by the scruff and hauls me up and over. I roll into a heap in the wet grass, gasping and flexing my stinging fingers. The night sky glitters overhead in an endless scape of stars—until a face appears above me, blocking it out.

It's a woman, hooded, leathery, the kind of person who looks much older than she probably is. Vivienne appears next, chattering happily to the woman in Ariminthian as she helps me sit up.

For a moment, all I can do is slump. I'm soaked to the skin, and the climb wrung out any last wisp of strength I had.

"Is she the lighthouse keeper?" I whisper to Vivienne. "I thought it would be a man."

"It's almost all women who are bound to the villa. The Royal Mother prefers it that way. They don't have families of their own, so they don't mind that it can be lonely." She lowers her voice and adds, "You will want to stay quiet while we're here. This lighthouse keeper has no liking for Durans. Her sons all died in the war."

"Yeah," I murmur, because I could say the same thing about my mom. It must be hard to be a mom when there's a war on. All you can do is worry and do your war work.

That's probably why Parliament sets everyone up with war work and doesn't give you a choice. *Stay busy. Don't let yourself start thinking about the situation you're in.* Or you might start to wonder why we're even still fighting a stupid war.

Is it so different where you're from? Or just dressed up better?

The lighthouse keeper gives us bread and tea, then blankets to sleep in near the fire. I keep my Duran mouth shut, smile a lot, and in return she avoids eye contact and leaves me alone and doesn't kill me in my sleep.

The next morning, I awaken in a stiff ball of agony. The lighthouse keeper is gone and Vivienne is already up, drinking tea and pacing. While we eat the bread the keeper left out, I tell Vivienne what the rowboat captain would have us do.

She's gotten much better at talking, so when she wordlessly puts down her bread and presses both hands to her face, a little dart of panic goes through me.

"Viv?" I keep my voice steady, but my heart is pounding.

"I have always done what's been asked of me. Even when it was more than what *should* have been asked." Vivienne swallows hard. "This time I can't. She wants me to forgive him and I can't."

I grip my teacup with both hands. *She* is the princess, and Vivienne doesn't question her wishes, whims, or instructions.

Ever.

He must be—

"My father," Vivienne goes on in a fierce whisper. "He made choices. I paid for them. Now his choices have brought peace. As if those choices were right all along, and disagreeing with them makes *me* the traitor."

"If there's amnesty for the pirates, neither one of you has to pay the price anymore," I reply carefully.

"You agree with the princess," she growls. "You think I should forgive my father."

I put my cup down, slow, deliberate, so it doesn't even clink. "I don't know what you should do. I just know I'd do pretty much anything to even *see* my dad again."

Vivienne lets out a long, shuddery breath.

"When someone is gone, what's already happened is all there is. I don't *get* to forgive my dad. Or give my mom a chance to make things right. I can't ask to hear their side. Or tell them off once and for all." I meet Vivienne's eye across the rickety table. "Your dad is still here. You can do any of those things. Or all of them. Or none of them. But you *can*. There are still things that you can make happen."

Vivienne mumbles something about service and the palace and a debt. She is sitting very still.

"Isn't that what we're doing here, trying to make something

happen? Trying to save the treaty?" I ask quietly. "We could just say *screw it* and walk away. You could go back to braiding hair, and I could, I don't know, sneak into Dura and wipe noses in the nursery, and the treaty would just be *gone*. We'd be at war again, and it'd be a billion years before anyone on either side breathes the word *treaty* in public, much less thinks there ought to be one."

Vivienne studies the table.

"But we're not doing that. Are we?" I wait till she looks at me. "No one liked the treaty because it meant no one won the war. But that means no one *lost*, either. If there's peace, it doesn't mean anything has been forgiven. Or has to be forgiven. It just means we're moving forward."

Vivienne runs a thumb over the royal seal still tied to her wrist. The red gash under the string looks like raw meat, shiny and open.

"Let's move forward," she says.

In moments, we're out the door, down a path, and into a cheerful little woodland. She seems to know where we're going, and I get the sense she'd rather I stay quiet, which isn't easy, but I can't do any of this without her.

Vivienne keeps calling the Royal Mother's house a *villa*, which doesn't quite translate into the common language, so I'm not sure what to expect. Something grand for sure. If you have a bunch of kids with a king, you're going to live somewhere nice, even if you're not married to him.

But the building Vivienne steers us toward isn't a monstrosity with white marble pillars and acres of manicured grounds. The house is stately and made of gleaming wood, but it's surrounded by pastures with simple four-board fences. It looks like a picture in one of the books I'd read to kids in the nursery, something with a title like *The House in the Country*.

Vivienne doesn't bother with the front door. Instead she heads straight for a big, sprawling building a short way from the house. There are water troughs outside, covered porches crammed with bales of hay, and several horses grazing in a field behind it. Inside there's a row of big box stalls that open to the pasture. The ceiling is high and the whole place feels airy and clean, even though it smells like animals.

There's a woman with her back to us standing in the wide aisle. She's wearing old trousers and a big floppy hat, and she's brushing a brown horse that's tied to a hook on one of the stalls.

Vivienne breaks away from me, hurrying. She's clawing at her wrist, trying to free the royal seal. The woman turns just in time for Vivienne to collapse at her feet, sobbing too hard to speak.

I have the sudden, awkward realization that I am in the presence of the Royal Mother of Ariminthia.

Vivienne is kneeling, cowering, curled like a bug but holding the royal seal above her bent head with both hands, pleading as if her life depends on it.

The Royal Mother takes the little golden object from Vivienne. Her eyes widen, and she looks from the seal to Vivienne and back, then she calmly drops the seal into her pocket and puts one arm around Vivienne's shoulders, helping her stand.

"Now then," the Royal Mother says in the common language. Her voice is soothing and gentle, like she's talking to a jittery horse. "Why don't you both come inside and tell me everything."

VIVIENNE

TELL ME EVERYTHING.

We do. Well, Cora does. Even the parts that make her look bad.

I sit with my hands folded tightly, perched on a wooden chair in the Royal Mother's sitting room.

The Royal Mother and my mistress have the same heart-shaped face. The same thick, wild eyebrows. It's like looking into a mirror that sees a future my mistress will never have, and it fills my whole self with a heavy kind of pain that's hard to think through.

But this is what the princess wanted me to do, whatever the cost, and I've done it.

I am picturing what it would be like, my father and me in that little house by the wharf. If there was peace, if there was amnesty, he could go back to the sea, hauling in a catch or loading cargo for some foreign port, and I could be the one by the window sewing sea bags for merchants and scientists, not soldiers. Each night we'd eat supper at that old table in the kitchen while the tide gently rolled beneath us.

It would not be the same, but it would be something.

Cora keeps talking. The Royal Mother listens calmly. Her eyes fill with tears once or twice, but she does not interrupt.

It would not be forgiveness, but it would be moving forward.

A silence has fallen. Cora is sitting on the edge of a pink chaise longue, her leg bouncing with a kind of nervous energy that she can't seem to contain. She seems to be bracing for something.

"Well." The Royal Mother holds the seal in her lap with both hands, like it's a baby bird. "I don't know what to say. This is a lot to take in."

Cora's leg abruptly stops bouncing. "We brought you this thing. Say you're going to use it."

The Royal Mother frowns the smallest bit, like she's not used to someone speaking to her so plainly. "It's not that simple. Right now, I'm not the regent of Ariminthia. The minister for counterterrorism is."

"Okay." Cora leans forward. "He made himself regent, right? No one else decided that. Why can't you do the same? Only make it official?"

The Royal Mother looks thoughtful. "He did not have a convocation, that is true."

"And he doesn't have the seal," I say, and when both of them look at me, I fight the urge to study my feet.

The Royal Mother turns the seal over and over in her hands. "If I issue writs to the noble lords summoning them into my presence for a proper convocation, they will have two choices: refuse to respond to a document bearing the royal seal of Ariminthia—which is treason—or come here in their robes of state and submit to my authority and recognize me as regent instead of Ingannaro."

Cora pumps her fist in some kind of victory gesture. "Yeah! Let's do that!"

"The noble lords would have to sail through the minister's blockade, and I don't imagine Ingannaro would let them pass without a fight," the Royal Mother reminds her. "They cannot come up the emergency ladders. It would have the look of cowardice."

"They wouldn't have to fight if the antiwar pirates clear out that blockade," Cora says.

The Royal Mother wrinkles her nose. She did not seem surprised to learn those the palace has long branded as pirates and punished as traitors are antiwar volunteers, but she clearly does not relish the thought of collaborating with them.

"You need the nobility onside, right? At least most of them. That's what Vivienne says." Cora tips her chin at me, and when the Royal Mother follows the gesture, I don't know where to look. "Viv also told me you'd sign a peace treaty once you're regent. Seal it. With the seal. That you have now. See? Simple."

The Royal Mother almost smiles. "Assuming the noble lords acknowledge me as regent and I have the authority to set this seal to a treaty, there remains your government. Frankly, I don't believe they'd accept the terms of the treaty now, even though they were ready to accept them only a few weeks ago."

The dark look about her suggests there is more she'd like to add about Durans and their trustworthiness and general character, but she's refraining out of courtesy.

"Yeah. I get why you'd think that." Cora brushes at a muddy spot on the chaise left by her trousers. "But there's a way forward, if you know how to work it. And if we're lucky."

The Royal Mother frowns in bewilderment. "Work . . . it?"

"You know how Dura's got two main political parties, right? Well, since the *Burying Ground* has been lost, right now they're fighting one another over who gets to be in charge. Let's say you publicly announce that you'll sign a peace treaty on behalf of Ariminthia. Seal it. Whatever. One of those parties is going to say *no freaking way*. The other is going to be willing to talk, just because their opposition hates the idea."

The Royal Mother's frown deepens. She seems to be translating several times in her head, which feels very familiar.

"That . . . does not make a lot of sense," she finally says.

Cora laughs. "No, it doesn't, does it? But here's how it could go: Ariminthia offers Dura something worthwhile. Something you're willing to give when the time comes, but something the party you offer it to can't easily turn down.

If they accept, that's peace, everyone! But if they *do* turn it down, you leak everything to the press, and that party will get a proper shellacking in the papers and lose face and probably the next election, which could very well be called immediately as a vote of no confidence."

"I knew there was a reason I live on an island, away from all this nonsense," the Royal Mother murmurs, running her thumb over the seal.

"But here's the magical part!" Cora goes on. "The party who originally didn't want to sign a treaty with you? They'll suddenly be interested in knowing more. They'll review the offer you made and decide it's *to the advantage of Dura* to sign it. They'll be the ones who brought peace to Dura after so long, and the other party, well . . ."

Cora opens her hands in a gesture that suggests the fate of the other party will not be worth considering.

"That brings us back to the question of the noble lords of Ariminthia," the Royal Mother says to her. "Ingannaro is an important man. He has at least some of the lords of the admiralty on his side or there wouldn't be a blockade of my doorstep. He has an actual blood claim to the throne, even if it's faint. All I can ever be is regent."

Cora lifts her chin. "Vivienne told me that her princess hated the war and wanted peace. You were her mom. No, scratch that—you *are* her mom. Just because she's dead doesn't change that fact. You will *always* be her mom."

The Royal Mother blinks hard and fast. My heart sinks

like an anchor, down and down, because *dead* has sharp Duran corners and her grief must still be raw.

"She wanted peace," Cora repeats, "and you can make that happen for her. The counterterrorism minister is some big shot—so what? You are the *Royal Freaking Mother*, and moms do *not* mess around when it comes to their kids. Also? I might not know a lot about monarchies, but I *do* know that you have *royal* in your title and he does not. He's just some dude with a government job."

"He's not just—" The Royal Mother sighs but tries to smile. "Oh, child. You are making this sound almost possible."

"Well." Cora shuffles her feet in the pile carpet. "I need it to be possible. You're pretty much my last hope."

The minister for counterterrorism would put Cora in the cage nearest to shore, where the sun would bake her into madness and the seabirds would pick her helpless flesh to ribbons for an eternity before the sea could draw its merciful veil over her.

The Royal Mother nods, slow and thoughtful. "I hope you can appreciate that I'm going to need time to make good decisions. For now, I don't know how to put this politely, but you don't smell very nice. I've had the maids prepare you a bath, and they'll put out some clean clothes for you once you're finished."

"Oh man, thank you!" Cora grins. "But you know what? Can I have these clothes back? The ones I'm wearing? I mean, you can *wash* them—or, probably have someone else wash them, because yeah, they *really* need to be washed—but I kind of inherited them and they can't just get thrown out."

It's a small thing. Very small. She might not even know that a dead person's possessions hold part of them and must be handled with care.

For some reason, it matters to her. Even though she's Duran.

"Of course." The Royal Mother pulls a bell rope and a girl appears. Cora follows the maid down the hall and around the corner. Once their footsteps fade, it's just the Royal Mother and me.

"How much of that is true?" the Royal Mother asks. "You may sp—"

"All of it." I shift on the wooden chair. "That is, obviously I don't know what went on before we met on the island, or after she was taken from the *Raptor*, but the rest is as she said."

Even as I'm saying it, I realize what I did.

I spoke over the Royal Mother of Ariminthia in my own voice.

"Well, one thing is clear. I believe you. I believe the sea and that island and Au-Aubrey . . ." She takes a moment and masters herself. "Aubrey. I believe they worked together to ensure you arrived here with this seal. For good or ill, I am meant to rule."

Something warm and expansive fills my whole self, at first puffing out my chest and then gathering behind my eyes, like tears on the edge of spilling over.

"I just . . . don't know where to begin." The Royal Mother holds the seal up to the light. "I'm still getting used to the fact that they're gone. All of them. All at once. I'll never see any of them again." She wipes away tears at the same time she smiles wryly. "Perhaps I should ask your Duran friend. She does not seem to be lacking in initiative."

I snort a little laugh. Cora is lacking in many things, but initiative is not one of them.

Cora would just say what she thinks. She only has one voice—her own.

"May I make a suggestion?" I touch my bare, throbbing wrist, and when the Royal Mother nods, I go on. "You will need to make a decision about the antiwar volunteers. We must send a signal at the next full moon if you plan to accept their help."

The Royal Mother scowls. "I don't see how I can refuse. Unfortunately."

"Not unfortunate for me," I say in a small voice. "Amnesty would mean my family's debts are paid in full."

The Royal Mother's face changes. Quietly she says, "I'd forgotten."

My eyes are filling with tears, and I'm trembling because saying the words out loud makes them real.

No more debts. I'll be free.

"You are of course welcome to stay in royal service," the Royal Mother goes on. "You could even have a position here at the villa if you'd like."

Her voice is kindly. She is offering a gift. When you're not a debtor, royal service means food and lodging and a community around you. For someone whose parents made the decisions mine did, it would be a lifeline.

I smile. For what feels like the first time in years and years.

"Thank you," I tell the Royal Mother of Ariminthia, "but I think I need to move forward."

CORA

I TAKE THREE baths in a row. The first is to scrub away the layers and layers of grime. The second is to be sure the dirt is really gone. The third is just to soak in, to feel safe and warm and kind of normal.

I'm not sure what to expect once I get out and put on the dress that's been left draped over a chair. Technically we're still at war. The Royal Mother could send me to the dungeon. Something worse than the brig of the *Raptor* or the gatehouse of Tideland Dock.

Instead I'm shown to a guest room where the girl who drew my bath brings food on a silver tray. A *whole meal*, with meat and bread and vegetables and a freaking *cake*. Not a cockle or a daleberry in sight.

I eat every crumb, hide the red pirate mirror under my pillow, then sleep for what feels like days. It might actually be days, since when I wake up, my clothes from before are carefully folded on a chair by the window, and there's another huge meal sitting on the table getting cold.

Once I'm full, I pick up my old camisole and underwear from the dress shop. They're faded and falling apart, but I put them on anyway. They don't remind me of Kess anymore. They remind me of being a normal kid, someone with a mom who flipped out over lacy underpants.

Alivarda's shirt and trousers are soft and clean like they never were on the island. They've become such a part of me that it's hard to put on the dress I was given, but there's no reason to be a jerk about a gift. I leave his kit folded on the chair where I can see it, then slide the pirate mirror into the pocket of my dress.

I don't think I'm a prisoner, but I am still technically a war criminal. I don't know what I'm allowed to do, or what I'm supposed to do or *not* supposed to do, but I'm not good at sitting still, so I drift down the corridors and accidentally on purpose glance into sitting rooms and cloister gardens just to take my bearings.

Someone clearly notices, because it's not long before the girl who drew my bath stops me mid-hallway and tells me that the Royal Mother would like to see me.

The girl shows me to a courtyard where the Royal Mother is drinking tea in the shade. I cautiously take the seat that the girl pulls out for me.

"How are you feeling?" The Royal Mother pushes a plate of sandwiches in my direction.

"Better." Even though I just ate, I grab a sandwich and take a bite. I grin with my mouth full when I taste that fish paste from the safe house, and I hope that the CO is okay, wherever he is.

"I've decided that I will allow the pir— ah, the antiwar volunteers to support my regency."

I fight an eye roll. She'll *allow* it. But it's good news, so I just nod cheerfully with my mouth full and let the pompousness go.

"The moon will be full in two weeks' time. Please be prepared to send whatever signal will be required." The Royal Mother can't quite hide her reluctance. "With that in mind, we need to discuss your future. Things are going to start happening quickly once the pirates break the blockade and I can parley with them directly."

The Royal Mother is taking their help. She is going to compromise.

"Once there's open water to the mainland," the Royal Mother goes on, "I will ferry over a scribe who will produce the necessary writs to summon the noble lords to convocation." She gestures, and the girl pours me a cup of tea. "We'll see how many will come."

"That's the thing that will make you regent?" I ask.

"That is the *holy rite* that will signify that the noble lords acknowledge my authority, yes." She smiles halfway. "The common language is deeply inelegant at times."

I translate until I get *weird*, then I smile back.

"If convocation is a success, I will immediately move to the palace on the mainland. The noble lords who convened will accompany me, along with the pirate fleet, and—please the ocean—the lords of the admiralty and the bulk of the Ariminthian navy." The Royal Mother sips her tea. Her hands tremble on the cup. "It will either be a triumphal procession or the opening salvo of a civil war."

I nod, because it seems like the wrong time to ask about a pardon.

"If it's civil war, well." She shrugs. "That's that. But if my regency holds, the very first thing I will do is pursue peace. That is what my Aubrey wanted, why she has made all of this happen, and I owe it to her to at least try."

I can't help but wonder if my own mother would do the same. If she could choose peace without victory in spite of everything she lost.

"I've been thinking about what you said when you first arrived," the Royal Mother goes on. "How I might best . . . *work it.*"

I sit up straighter. I'm not used to adults listening when I talk. I'm *definitely* not used to adults taking me seriously.

"My first act as regent will be to send emissaries to Dura, letting them know that Ariminthia is ready to seal a treaty that is identical to the previous one, but for one additional concession: Ariminthia agrees to Dura's claims to all the islands where it's currently operating mining colonies. Only new colonies will have to be registered."

My brows go up. "That is . . . a big concession."

"Something Dura wants that I'm willing to give. Much as it pains me." She looks away, into the courtyard. "I will also agree to personally travel to Dura and seal the treaty with my own hand, in the Parliament building. No ships. No neutral ports. Also, with as many reporters as they want present to witness the event."

The Royal Mother's face is serene, but I know she's hiding a scowl. Getting the Ariminthians to agree to even one reporter on the *Burying Ground* was a major point of contention.

"You'd go yourself?" I ask. "You *trust* them?"

She doesn't answer right away, and in that moment I realize I didn't say *us*. I said *them*.

"Someone must be the first," the Royal Mother says quietly.

I think about the island, how Vivienne stood at the bottom of that tree looking up and up as I climbed.

How I tied knots in that rope for the enemy.

"So . . . what does this have to do with me?" I ask.

"I imagine you'd like to return to Dura," she says. "Joining me would provide an opportunity for you to have an escort back to your homeland. You'd have a full royal pardon, of course. For form's sake."

On the island, that was all I wanted—to arrive home to parades and galas and celebrations and fetes. I wanted everyone to crowd around me, to beg and clamor to hear my story.

Back when I was a hero survivor of the *Burying Ground* who used her wits and training to overcome all odds.

"Cora?" The Royal Mother's voice is quiet. "Don't you want to go home?"

It's a gray house, the shutters painted the color of cake

batter. My room is at the back, overlooking a little yard where my old swing set still creaks on windy days. The war department would never let me stay there, not on my own. Off I'd go into the war orphans program, and it wouldn't be somewhere good like the fish hatchery.

It wouldn't be somewhere I'd ever choose to go.

"I understand your parents were on the *Burying Ground*. I'm sorry for your loss." The Royal Mother turns her teacup back and forth in its saucer. "You don't have to return to Dura right away if you don't want to."

It's not that I don't want to go back. I want to go back to before that ship sailed. Before the prime minister's lottery chose my dad to report on the treaty. Maybe before the war ever started, even though that was way before I was born. Before I knew what Parliament was capable of.

I want to be Before Cora, who wiped noses in the nursery and missed her friends and had big dreams about a stupid fish hatchery.

"If I stayed here . . ." I hesitate. "It would be weird, wouldn't it?"

"You would be granted political asylum and given refugee status." She manages a smile. "Perhaps you might become my cultural adviser. I know so little of Dura, and what I do know isn't . . . positive."

I eat another sandwich, then another one. If my mouth is full, I don't have to talk. I don't have to explain that I don't want to return to a country that was prepared to let me die, and I don't want to stay in one that was prepared to kill me.

I just want to be a regular kid. I want to complain about my chores and get in trouble for staying out late.

Like Vivienne gets to, now that there's going to be an amnesty.

"I should thank you," I finally say to the Royal Mother. "For the food and the bath and everything, but mostly for believing us."

She toys with her teacup some more, then gestures for the serving girl to leave. Once we're alone, she says, "I do believe you. I wouldn't be pursuing this course of action otherwise. But something's not right. The reason we build with springwood is because the sea will not take it. When we build a ship, we burn its name into every plank because we know the sea will spit them back. Those planks will wash up where we can find them, and we can mourn and make the proper offerings."

On the island, I found rope and sailcloth. Alivarda's canvas sea bag and the leather valise.

Nothing made of wood. Not a single splinter.

"There should be *wreckage*." The Royal Mother's voice shakes. "Why has *no one* found any wreckage?"

The counterterrorism minister oversaw the ship's construction, and now there's no royal family, and he thinks to make himself king and reject the treaty and keep us from getting their maps. Parliament didn't like how the treaty required all mining colonies to be registered and regulated, and they commissioned a special table made of decorative ironwork with graceful hollow legs and metal spikes hammered deep into the deck for the grip.

I put my teacup down. It makes a tiny, shuddery *clink*.

I don't know much about ships and boats and storms and currents, but the Royal Mother is right.

There should be wreckage.

VIVIENNE

CORA LEARNS I'VE been lodged in the servants' quarters. She crashes in full of outrage, yelling how I don't belong there, how I can stay in her room if I want to, that I'm a regular kid now and not a servant anymore and on and on.

It's a kind gesture, but she seems to have forgotten that we are not in the jungle any longer and she has no more authority than I do. Until the Royal Mother sets that seal to an amnesty and a pardon, I still belong to the palace and Cora is still a war criminal.

Besides, it was never the work I minded.

The full moon comes around. Cora makes enough noise that the Royal Mother's chatelaine permits me to go with her to the lighthouse, and we make our way there in the darkest part of night in the company of a sturdy groundskeeper. Sure enough, there are five winks of red light that answer ours.

Less than a week later, we awaken to the smell of grapeshot.

Cora blows into the yard where I'm hanging laundry and all but drags me toward the cliffs. "Come with me. I need to know if this is good or bad."

The elevator station overlooks the stretch of water that separates the Royal Mother's island from the mainland. Below, in the harbor, the blockade is in disarray as a solid wall of pirate vessels streams from either headland. There are sloops and warships and even the dreadnought *Victory*, which we were told was lost with all hands almost a year ago.

"The antiwar volunteers are breaking up the blockade," I tell her. "It may look like a battle, but it's not. The pirate vessels outnumber those loyal to the minister for counter-terrorism, and most of their shots must have been across the bow—warning shots—because Ingannaro's captains are standing down. Do you see? They're shifting the colors to a quarter staff. That means they aren't surrendering, but they also won't attack."

"That's . . . good?"

"That's *very* good. It means they're not willing to risk their crews for a fight they know they can't win. It means they haven't been told to feed the sea. To die here."

Cora cranes her neck for a better look. "I was kind of hoping one of the ships would get hit with a cannonball. I wanted to see what would happen to the wood."

I turn and start back to the villa, but she grabs my arm just long enough to stop me.

"Someone else can hang the wash. Right?" Cora's voice is quiet, almost small. Cora's voice is never quiet or small. "I thought we could watch this."

I translate a few times. "I must do the tasks assigned to me. You have no chores because you're a guest."

She laughs mirthlessly. "Right. A servant and a guest. Might as well get used to it now, right?"

"Not for too much longer," I reply. "The pirates will arrive at the villa before day's end. There will be a delegation and probably a scribe, and they will insist the amnesty be the first document the Royal Mother issues once her regency begins."

Cora doesn't say anything.

"I'm sure the second document will be your pardon," I add, because Cora not saying anything is unsettling. "Along with orders for a ship to sail you to Dura. You must be looking forward to going home."

"It's . . . complicated." She says it quietly, almost in a palace voice. "But it's not going to be like that."

"You will be . . . staying here? In Ariminthia?"

Cora hitches a shoulder. She is still watching the pirate fleet scatter the vessels belonging to the minister for counter-terrorism. The blue of the harbor and the pale bleached canvas of the sails. The sharp timber spars and crisp uniforms.

Her eyes are shiny.

It slowly dawns on me, what she's saying.

Everything she has done—everything *we* have done—every

sacrifice, every pain and terror—Cora did them all for no reward but peace.

It might be the least Duran thing I have ever seen her do.

If it's true that something is keeping her from her homeland, if she really must stay here, she will be one of a very few Durans in the entire realm, and probably the only Duran girl.

My mistress could not sleep without a lamp burning. Sometimes in the night, she would dip her toe off the foot of the bed and gently brush my shoulder, just to make sure I was still there.

We did not have a lot in common, the princess and I, but each of us knew what it was to feel alone.

It's a lot for my mistress to ask of anyone. Cora will have nothing of her old life to see her safely through. She will not have the luxury of holding to old ways of thinking. She will need to wake up each morning and choose peace actively, with intent, and live it.

Perhaps Cora is not the only one meant to move forward in this way.

"Well." I glance at her sidelong. "You know where my house is. If you are ever hungry for cockles."

Cora turns to me. She is grinning in spite of her reddened eyes. "Ha! Maybe. Tell you what. I'll bring the fish paste sandwiches."

CORA

THINGS HAPPEN FAST, just like the Royal Mother said.

I hardly notice, though. I'm stuck on how many things about the loss of the *Burying Ground* don't add up.

The pirates send a scribe. He arrives in the first boat with the delegation. It's pretty clear that the Royal Mother would rather choose one herself, but there's also no graceful way for her to insist. She sets him up at a desk in the sunroom, and before he does anything else, he drafts a proclamation of general amnesty and leaves it where she'll see it each time she walks past. Two days later, there's a stack of writs that go out to the Ariminthian nobility, requesting them to come to the island for convocation.

Vivienne and I weren't found in the agreed-upon signing area. The wind from the storm might have blown the *Burying Ground* off course. But what if the captain intentionally steered the ship wrong? What if someone in one of the delegations messed with his compass?

Well-dressed men arrive, several each day, until there are dozens of them. Vivienne calls them *noble lords* and stays well clear of them. One afternoon, they and the Royal Mother and the scribe shut themselves in the great hall and bar the doors. I'm not invited—fair enough—so I don't know what exactly happens, but when they come out, the Royal Mother is officially the regent of Ariminthia.

The Ariminthians were so sure I'd sabotaged the *Burying Ground*. Their high court was ready to pronounce sentence before I even got there. Not even servants who braid hair would believe a storm could sink so grand a vessel, not when the captain of the *Raptor* was so adamant. The Ariminthians know their own ships, and no one in charge had any reason to suspect one of their own, even if he had every opportunity and also a motive.

Springwood is supposed to be this perfect watertight, salt-resisting miracle wood, something it would take *some doing* to compromise. Maybe it takes less doing right from the start, as you're building some giant warship that you've given a name like the *Burying Ground*.

I know next to nothing about ships in general, much less Ariminthian ships, but even I know one shouldn't fall apart under you if there's a storm. And I'm pretty sure whatever's left shouldn't be oily to the touch.

Maybe it doesn't matter. The Royal Mother receives a report that Ingannaro has vacated the palace and retreated to his estate. Several more nobles arrive sheepishly late, making excuses for missing convocation. The admiralty sends a warship escort for her procession across the strait.

It looks like there's going to be peace.

That's got to mean something, right? That's got to mean that Parliament wouldn't care if I went home, especially if I promised to keep a low profile. That's got to mean kids won't have to do war work anymore, although it's hard to know what that would look like.

I can't even imagine what else I could do. School, maybe. If you believe the old-timers, kids used to go to school till they were much older than twelve, and school had things like clubs and art and dances, but that all got scrapped because even kids can't be wasting time on useless things when there's a war.

On the morning of the procession, it takes a long, boring time to shuttle everyone down the elevator. There are all these complicated rules about who gets to go first and which lord is important enough to ride in the elevator cage with some other lord. Apparently, this stuff *matters*, but there's going to be peace so I'm trying not to be too annoyed.

No one's sure what to do with me, since I'm sort of a guest but also still an unpardoned war criminal, so I crowd in with the underchef and two laundresses, and no one can think of a reason why that's wrong. The cables creak ominously as the elevator cage grinds its way down the cliff face, but it's nowhere near as bad as climbing a soaking rope ladder at night, so I smile the whole way.

The servants have been busy since daybreak, loading barges with bags and trunks, but that's not where I spot Vivienne. She's climbing into a little rowboat nudged between the larger vessels and taking a seat next to a hooded figure, who promptly pushes off with a dripping paddle and rows steadily into the chaos toward the mainland.

Oh.

That must be her dad. The amnesty has been drafted but not sealed—the Royal Mother wants to issue all official documents from the Cerulean Throne to make her regency extra-official—but I don't blame Vivienne one bit for not wanting to risk going back to the palace.

I start to wave to her, then think better of it. Best to let her go. I know where to find her.

The palace isn't all marble and stone like the newspapers said. Instead it's made of wood—all kinds and shades, rich, elegant, polished to a shine. It is big, though, and since I haven't been told where I can and can't go, I hang around outside the spacious office that used to be the king's, that the Royal Mother—the *regent*, now—has taken over.

I spend a month that way, then two.

Ministers come and go, along with messengers from the admiralty and different commanders from the front. I learn several important things:

The peace delegation has been dispatched to Dura, along with the treaty that includes the new concession.

The cease-fire seems to be holding despite the loss of the

Burying Ground. It's like everyone on both sides is holding their breath. Or perhaps more people are ready to embrace peace than the newspapers wanted us to believe.

There is still no word on any other survivors.

That's the thing weighing on me now. Vivienne and I were found where no one thought to look. Who's to say there aren't others? The CO said the pirates were the only people looking for survivors. What if the antiwar coalition disbands because there's no more war, but both Dura and Ariminthia decide that peace means there's no reason to search?

"Cora." The Royal Mother appears in the doorway of the office, frowning slightly. "Was there something you need?"

"Oh!" I leap up from the bench, caught in the act. Even though I'm not doing anything. "No. That is. I was . . . hoping to borrow paper and ink. I'd like to write a letter."

She steps into the room, gesturing that I should follow. I have no one to write to, but the Royal Mother doesn't know that, and it's better than admitting I was lurking a little.

There are four portraits on the wall behind the big desk. Three girls and a boy, each painted when they were around my age.

I never really looked at any of the royal children while we were on the *Burying Ground*. I never thought of them as kids like me.

Maybe they're out there, too, on some island, hoping someone will find them so they can hug their mom the way I really, *really* hope I can hug mine.

The pirate scribe looks up as the Royal Mother approaches his desk. It's a condition of her agreement with the antiwar league that he writes and reviews every document she issues. She asks if he has any paper to spare. It's hard to come by in Ariminthia, and he has to hunt for it.

As he's sifting through messy stacks on the desk, there's a clatter in the hallway that gets louder until four men trample into the room, talking over one another wildly in Ariminthian. It's so sudden and they're so keyed up that I'm sure it's an assassination attempt, but they kneel around the Royal Mother before bouncing to their feet like toys in the bath, still gabbling.

"Gentlemen!" The Royal Mother holds up her hands. "My lords of the admiralty. One at a time, and in the common language, for our scribe. Please."

For our scribe. More like so the scribe—and therefore the pirates—can be sure that the Royal Mother isn't trying to keep secrets.

The lord of the northern seas fidgets with a blocky silver ring. "Ma'am. Our treaty delegation has returned. The news is not good. The Durans refused to even let our emissaries on their soil. They said that we violated the terms of the cease-fire, and thus that a state of active hostility exists between our countries. They gave the delegation two hours to leave the area before they sent war machines after us."

"But why?" The Royal Mother's voice is sharp. "What happened?"

The lord of the western seas pulls at his beard. "Because of you, ma'am."

"The moment the Durans learned you were the one who sent the delegation, they demanded to know why you were not on the *Burying Ground*," says the lord of the southern seas. "They refused to even look at the treaty and its new concession. They wanted to know why Ariminthia had a member of the royal family to put on the throne."

"But I—I'm *not* part of the royal family," the Royal Mother stammers, "and I'm not on the throne. And besides, they must have *known* that already. Who and what I was. I have no claim to the throne. I am the *regent!*"

"The emissaries brought that up," says the lord of the northern seas, "but things got . . . contentious."

The Royal Mother sinks into the nearest chair. She puts a hand to her forehead.

"The Durans formally accused us of sinking the *Burying Ground*," says the lord of the eastern seas. "They claim that leaving out a member of the royal family, in direct violation of the agreement, was proof that we planned the catastrophe. We would have a monarch on the throne while they scrambled to elect a new slate of functionaries."

"It was a *storm!*" I snap, even though I'm honestly not sure that's the root of it anymore. Everyone turns toward me, and I know I should keep quiet but I don't care. "Didn't the emissaries tell the Durans that?"

The lord of the southern seas looks like he swallowed too big a bite of something rotten. "They . . . ah . . . the Duran government doesn't believe there are any eyewitnesses. They claim you're an impostor being paid by the Crown to say the lines we're feeding you. About the storm, about being so far off course, about the ship falling apart."

I'm stammering. I don't know what to say, and I *always* have something to say.

The Royal Mother is studying me through narrowed eyes, and I belatedly realize that I was the one who assured her a concession would work. Someone had to be the first, but because she took that risk—at the word of a Duran, one with a wild and improbable story that no one can prove and who is also the right age to be a saboteur—the Royal Mother's regency, her *authority*, just took a massive hit.

It should have worked. Parliament had every reason to accept the treaty, especially with that plump new concession.

Unless they never wanted peace in the first place.

"Well." The Royal Mother stands up, graceful and arrow straight. She gestures, and the lords of the admiralty move closer. "Does this mean what I think it means?"

"That we're at war once again?" The lord of the northern seas sighs long and deep. "Yes, ma'am. We are. We must be."

The Royal Mother picks up the seal from the little box on her desk. She turns it over once, letting it catch a wink of light.

"I suppose Ingannaro gets his wish after all. It's almost as if he knew this would happen. I did wonder why he withdrew to his estate without a fight." She speaks quietly, to herself. "I'm sorry, Aubrey. You did your best."

The lords of the admiralty trade looks, and it's not the steely resolve you'd hope for. Rather, they look like they've bought the wrong size shoes at the market, and they're pretty sure the merchant won't exchange them.

"Right." The Royal Mother's voice isn't angry, but it's cold and firm. "Dispatch the fleet. Victory footing. We will meet in the war room in one turn of the glass."

"One thing before we go, ma'am." The lord of the eastern seas glances at me, then switches to Ariminthian. The Royal Mother frowns and responds, then the other lords chime in. Every now and then they look over at me, quick, like I'm different than I was ten minutes ago.

Something tugs at my sleeve. The pirate scribe quietly turns a sheet of paper toward me. On it he's made a quick sketch.

His eyes are huge and anxious, and he tips his chin at the lords of the admiralty and the Royal Mother.

Oh.

I never did get my pardon. Technically I'm still a war criminal, all but convicted of sinking the *Burying Ground* and murdering the whole royal family.

The Royal Mother says something in Ariminthian that must be an order, because the lords of the admiralty bow and disappear one after another like pallbearers.

I stand very still by the pirate scribe's desk. I'm putting the pieces together. Parliament never wanted peace. Neither did Ingannaro.

"Cora, I'm sorry." The Royal Mother moves to block the doorway. "I'm going to have to take you into custody."

"Why?" My voice goes high and sharp, almost a screech. "What's going to happen?"

"You're an enemy combatant now. Don't worry. It'll just be house arrest."

The pirate scribe slides the sketch into a pile of papers without a sound. I grip the edge of his desk. Otherwise I think I might collapse.

They'll have the trial now. Ariminthia will come together to see the assassin punished. Dura will rally to avenge what the papers will call a *barbarous act* and a *hallmark of injustice*.

"House arrest," I repeat, and the Royal Mother nods too quickly. Her smile just a beat too late.

"Not political asylum," I press.

"My regency is fragile enough as it is. The minister for counterterrorism is sure to mount a challenge. The realm knows about the king's brothers. I can't give the noble lords a reason to doubt their faith in me." She grips the royal seal. "War with Dura is one thing. This realm *will not* see a civil war. I owe my daughter that much."

Stay calm.

I do. My heart is racing, but I straighten and say, "Well, then. Guess I'd better go back to my room."

"Wait a moment. I must call a gendarme to escort you."

I may have been trained for all the wrong reasons, but that doesn't mean it was for nothing.

At this point there is no shame in anything you do.

The gendarme follows me to my room in the guest wing, then takes up watch outside. This chamber is bigger and nicer than my room at home—nicer than my whole *house* if I'm being honest—and decorated with paintings of sunsets over water.

I sit on the edge of the bed and breathe steadily and take my bearings.

One painting has a ship in it. It looks a little like the *Burying Ground*, with a bunch of masts and all kinds of sails and rope everywhere.

Peace might have meant that both Dura and Ariminthia gave up on the *Burying Ground*. Or it might have meant that both would try to figure out what happened to it. They'd go looking for survivors, and not in whatever cloak-and-dagger way the antiwar league has to do it. A full flotilla, with maps and charts and an organized, systemized strategy.

Someone *should* try to figure out what happened.

I pull the pirate mirror out of my pocket. The red glass gleams when I open the clamshell lid.

The amnesty for antiwar volunteers depended on peace. So much for Vivienne's chance to be an ordinary kid.

Probably she could come back to the safety of the palace, but I doubt she will. She'll be on the run, helping people climb through walls, easing herself silently through that hatch in her kitchen floor. She's a pirate now. Pirates make their own choices, and Vivienne is choosing her dad. She is choosing to be something *like* a normal kid.

Even if that's not something she gets to do for very long.

The pirates would probably take me in if I could make it to Vivienne's house. I have been trained for this. I would probably be very good at war.

Only I'm not. I can't be Kess, no matter what skivvies I'm wearing.

The war is starting again. There's too much for big shots to gain for things to be otherwise, and Dura's not the only one with this problem. It's not one you can fix with voting, either.

The treaty would have meant nobody won. Without it, we have all lost.

There are lots of ways to fight a war. One way is to pursue the truth. One way is to see what *is*, not what other people want you to see.

So maybe the pirates would help me search for the *Burying*

Ground. Maybe they would let me join a crew—or better yet, set me up with a little schooner and some like-minded people to help me learn to sail it.

We'd search for wreckage, and if there is none, we'll find out why. We'll look for signal fires and visible shacks, but more subtle signs, too.

We'd be far out on the high seas and far away from the war. Far from the nursery and the hatchery and the safe houses and the tidal cages.

Then I'd know. Not because it would mean medals and state dinners and standing in the spotlight as a hero Duran peacemaker. Not because it would make a difference to boys like my brothers and boys like Alivarda.

Because knowing will allow Before Cora to let go of what's never coming back, and knowing will let Now Cora become who she's meant to be.

Because knowing might make all the difference one day, when people are finally tired of big shots and their endless war.

I shuck off the dress and put on Alivarda's tunic and trousers. It won't fool anyone close up, but at a distance it might do some good. I drop the mirror in our pocket and press my ear against the door.

There is a very good chance that your enemy will underestimate you. There is a moment he will hesitate. That is your moment. Use it well.

You better believe I will.